Table of Contents

BORN BY THE FIRE

TOBY LAMAR YAWN

This is a work of fiction. Names, Characters, places, and incidents either are the product of the Author's imagination or are used fictitiously. Any resemblance to any actual person or persons, living or dead, events or locales is entirely coincidental.

ISBN: 979-8-9944188-0-2 (EBOOK)

ISBN: 979-8-9944188-1-9 (PAPERBACK)

YAWN ENTERTAINMENT PRESENTS A TOBY LAMAR YAWN NOVEL.

DEDICATION

To my friends and family.

ACKNOWLEDGMENTS

I want to acknowledge Andrew Klavan, whose advice on his podcast helped me write this story. I would like to recognize my brother, Chad Yawn, who spent countless hours reading my story and offering valuable suggestions. I would like to acknowledge my brother-in-law, Bradley Holt, who spent countless hours listening to me discuss writing and offering advice, both at work and at home

CHAPTER ONE

The first thing I saw was the torches. It was as if there were fifty living wounds of fire drifting through the black. They moved in perfect silence except for the hiss of burning pitch and the low pop when a knot of pine exploded in the flames. Our horses knew. Their ears flattened, nostrils flaring at the reek of kerosene and hate. One horse sidestepped, hooves skittering on gravel, but the line quickly reformed. The riders moved together until they felt less like individuals and more like a single creature, a pale serpent sliding down the dirt road with a hundred glowing eyes.

Nobody spoke. Nobody needed to.

Up front, my father sat straight as a judge on his big bay gelding. Ezekiel Whitlock never had to raise his voice; he only lifted his torch a fraction higher, and the entire column slowed to a crawl, hooves muffled in red dust, shadows stretching long and thin between the pines. Moonlight slid off the white hoods, turning them the color of old bone.

I could feel him from twenty yards back: the heat of his certainty rolling off him in waves, cold as well-water and twice as heavy. It pressed against my chest the way storm pressure before a twister touches ground. Every man there felt it too. You could see it in the way they held their reins, loose but ready, like men waiting for a sermon they already knew by heart.

Somewhere ahead, through the trees, a tiny house glowed soft and yellow, the last warm thing left in the world tonight, and we were coming for it.

We halted just beyond the last screen of pines. Down the gentle slope, the pastor's house sat lit from within, its windows spilling soft gold onto the grass, as if it still believed the world was gentle. A child's shadow crossed the curtain, small and quick, and something in my ribs cinched tight enough to hurt.

Ezekiel turned his horse in a slow, deliberate circle, the torch in his hand painting his hood the color of fresh blood. When he spoke, the words came low and sure, the same voice he used to read Scripture on Sunday mornings, only colder now, honed to a blade.

"Brothers," he said, not loud, but every man leaned forward to drink it in. "Tonight, we remind this county who owns its soul."

A ripple of assent moved through the line; torches lifted higher, a slow wave of fire.

"That preacher down there has forgotten the natural order," Ezekiel went on, pointing with the torch until the flames licked toward the little house.

"He fills their heads with poisonous ideas, tells 'em they're the same as us, tells 'em they can stand straight and look us in the eye. That's a sickness, brothers, and sickness has to be burned out before it spreads."

He let the silence settle, heavy as wet wool. Then he turned in the saddle and looked straight at me.

Jesse leaned over from his saddle; his hood tilted like a conspirator. Even through the cloth, I could hear the grin in his whisper.

"Go on, Caleb. Make your daddy proud."

The words slid into my ear like warm oil. I swung down. The ground felt suddenly foreign beneath my boots. My father was already there, waiting, the bottle cradled in his gloved hands like a newborn.

The rag hung limp and wet from the neck, reeking of gasoline. Torchlight painted the inside of his hood hell-orange, turning the eyeholes into empty sockets.

He held it out.

"Take it."

My fingers closed around the glass before my mind caught up. The bottle was heavier than sin and twice as cold. My hand shook; the liquid sloshed. Ezekiel saw; he always saw but said nothing. He only flicked a match alive between thumb and forefinger. The scratch cracked the night open like a rifle shot. Flame ran up the rag in a greedy blue tongue, and I was holding a living heart of fire.

"Strength before weakness," he said, soft enough that only I could hear. "Honor before softness. Blood before all."

A sermon in nine words. A death sentence in nine more.

Inside the house, a curtain twitched. I saw them plain: the pastor on his knees, arms around his wife; her face buried in her children's hair; the little boy's mouth open in a silent scream. Just a family. Just people. Praying to a God who was apparently busy elsewhere tonight.

My arm wouldn't move.

"What are you waiting for, boy?" My father's voice cut through the darkness cleanly. "Throw it."

The bottle burned hotter. The rag hissed against my wrist. My pulse was a drum that only I could hear, loud enough to rattle my bones.

"Caleb!"

The name cracked like a whip.

I threw it.

The bottle left my hand smooth and accurate, a comet trailing fire. It punched through the night and kissed the side of the house with a wet, glassy pop. Flame burst outward in a starving roar, licking up clapboards, hungry for more. The roar of approval rolled up from behind me, fifty hooded throats giving voice to something ancient and rotten.

Jesse's hand clapped my shoulder. "Attaboy," he laughed, giddy as a child on Christmas morning.

Then the screaming started.

Raw, animal, human. A sound that should never come out of a child. It poured through the broken window and wrapped around my throat like wire. My arms dropped. I couldn't move. The night narrowed to that single, impossible note.

Ezekiel raised both arms, torch high, a dark preacher baptizing the sky in smoke.

"Let this be a warning!" he thundered. "The Whitlock name does not know mercy!"

The men howled with him, a single savage creature drunk on its own voice.

The house burned brighter, hotter, painting us all the color of judgment. Black smoke clawed upward, thick and violent, blotting out the stars.

And in that moment, with the screams still climbing the night behind me, I understood I had just stepped across a line drawn in fire. My father would never let me step back. And I wasn't sure the boy who threw that bottle was still standing on this side of it.

CHAPTER TWO

I woke with the taste of smoke thick on my tongue, bitter and clinging like a confession I couldn't spit out. For a long minute, I lay still, eyes fixed on the cracked plaster ceiling, bargaining with God or fate or whatever listened to boys like me. Let it have been a nightmare. Let me wake up clean.

But nightmares don't settle into your bones like lead. They don't leave black flecks under my fingernails or the faint reek of kerosene in my hair. They don't make your chest feel hollowed out by something hotter than guilt.

I dragged myself upright and shuffled to the bathroom. The pull-chain bulb sputtered to life, weak and sickly yellow, the same light that had watched me grow up. I stopped dead in the doorway. The boy in the mirror was a stranger.

Caleb Whitlock. Eighteen. Six-one, broad across the shoulders from years of tossing hay bales and swinging an axe until my palms blistered. Father always said I carried myself like a man who knew his place. But the face staring back looked carved from ash, blond hair matted and wild, blue eyes gone pale and watery, ringed with bruise-colored shadows. My jaw was locked so tight the muscle jumped under the skin, and behind those eyes something dark moved, restless and hungry, something I refused to name.

I turned the tap hard. Cold water hit the basin like punishment. I cupped it, splashed my face again and again, scrubbing until my skin stung.

When I looked up, water dripping from my chin, nothing had changed. The stranger was still there, wearing my skin like a poorly fitted mask. A boy who had stood by while a house burned. Who could still hear children screaming.

"Caleb?" My mother's voice floated up the stairs, thin and careful, the way it got when Father wasn't home yet. "Breakfast is ready, sweetheart."

I pressed the towel to my face until the fibers burned my cheeks, then forced my feet to move. One step. Another. Down toward the smell of bacon and normalcy I no longer deserved.

BREAKFAST TABLE

The kitchen smelled of frying bacon and hot coffee, the kind of ordinary morning scent that used to mean the world was right-side up. Mama stood at the stove in her faded cotton apron, cinched tight around her narrow waist like she was holding herself together with it.

Annabelle Whitlock had always been small, barely taller than the enamel counter, and gentle as morning dew. When I was little, her smile came easily and often, lighting the whole room. These days, it only slipped out when Daddy was off at the factory or out with the men.

She turned when she heard me, and I saw what the night had done to her: eyes puffy and red-rimmed, like she'd cried herself dry after I'd gone to bed. She looked away quickly, poking at the eggs with a wooden spoon that trembled in her hand.

"Morning, Mama," I said, voice low.

She reached up and brushed my cheek with fingers that shook just a little. "You look worn out, sugar."

Before I could answer, heavy boots started down the stairs, slow, deliberate thuds that rattled the dishes in the cupboard. Daddy filled the doorway the way a thundercloud fills the sky: tall, thick through the chest, silver threading his beard, eyes hard and bright as busted glass. He carried the smell of last night's cigars and the cold woods on his clothes.

But this morning he was grinning wide, like a man who'd won something big.

"There's my boy!" he boomed, bringing his big hand down on my shoulder hard enough to sting. "Stood tall last night, Caleb. Show every man there you got Whitlock blood running true."

I kept my face still, though my stomach lurched and my heart climbed into my throat. He dropped into his chair, snapped open the newspaper, and slapped it on the oilcloth in front of me like he was proud to show off a trophy buck.

NEGRO PASTOR'S HOME GUTTED BY BLAZE

Below it, a picture of what was left: charred timbers and blackened walls staring empty as a picked-over carcass. The story said the preacher, his wife, and their girl got out with cuts and smoke in their lungs. But the little boy, four years old, had been carried out wrapped in a blanket, his skin burned badly. Doctors figured he'd live. Figured he'd hurt the rest of his days.

Daddy shoveled eggs into his mouth and talked around them. "That'll teach him," he muttered, satisfied. "Preaching that integration foolishness from the pulpit. Thinking he can stand up and talk equality to decent folks." He gave a short, ugly chuckle. "Maybe now his young'un'll know better about how the world's ordered."

My fork froze halfway to my mouth. He was proud, proud of me, for scaring a child for life.

Mama drifted over like a ghost, setting his toast down as carefully as setting nitroglycerin. One corner was a shade too dark.

Daddy's smile vanished. His voice dropped low, the way it did right before thunder. "This toast is burnt, woman. Are you trying to tell me something?"

"No, sir," she whispered, already reaching to take it back. "I'll fix another right now—"

His hand shot out, caught her wrist hard enough to whiten the skin. The flat of his other hand cracked across her backside, sharp, loud, mean as a whip. She stumbled forward a step but didn't cry out. Didn't even make a sound.

Something in me snapped loose.

"Dad!" The word tore out of me before I could stop it. I was half out of my chair.

He didn't even look at me. "Sit down, boy. A woman's place gets corrected when it needs correcting."

I sank back slowly, a thin, cold crack running straight through me, quiet but deep enough to change the shape of everything.

Mama kept her eyes on the toaster, hands shaking as she slid in fresh bread. She never once looked my way. She didn't have to. I could feel her hurt hanging in the air like a cloud of smoke.

"I need some air," I mumbled, pushing back from the table.

The sun climbed bright and clean over the cotton fields, just as always. Inside, my father was humming a hymn. Inside, my mother was making fresh toast. Inside, a four-year-old boy was waking up in a hospital with burns that would never fully heal. And I was standing between all of it, belonging nowhere.

CHAPTER THREE

The road to school stretched longer than usual that morning, the kind of quiet that rang in your ears and the bright that hurt to look at. Sunlight poured over the cotton fields like it was trying to wash the night clean, pretending nothing ugly had ever happened under its watch. Gravel popped under my boots, steady and indifferent. I shoved my hands deep in my pockets and tried to breathe the cool late-spring air without tasting smoke.

"Caleb Whitlock!" Jesse's voice cracked the silence behind me. "Slow them long legs down, boy!"

I turned just as he jogged up, grinning wide enough to split his freckled face. Jesse Boone looked built for trouble. Wiry, quick, all elbows and sharp corners, sandy hair sticking up like he'd combed it with a firecracker. Those green eyes of his always lit up at the first hint of mischief or meanness.

We'd been raised side by side, thick as thieves and twice as reckless. Fished the same creeks, took the same whippings, bled in the same dirt. The only difference was that Jesse still looked up to my daddy like he hung the moon. I, on the other hand, was starting to see the shadows it cast.

"Your old man gave a hell of a sermon last night," Jesse said, punching my arm hard enough to sting. "Shoot, Ezekiel Whitlock could talk fire outta green wood."

I managed a grunt. "Yeah."

"You're lucky, Caleb. My pa couldn't lead a prayer meeting, much less a chapter. I'd be strutting like a banty rooster if I had your blood."

He didn't notice how my shoulders locked up. Just kept walking, whistling some half-remembered Hank Williams tune, easy in his skin the way I used to be.

"You looked mean as hell throwing that bottle," he went on, nudging me. "Thought for a second you'd set the place ablaze just by glaring at it. C'mon, laugh, it's funny."

I forced a laugh. It came out thin, but it was enough. We fell into our old rhythm after that shoving, jawing about Jesse's sorry haircut, arguing whether Elvis could take Hank in a scrap. For a little while, it felt almost normal. Almost safe.

Then a motor roared behind us, rough and hungry. A beat-up '50 Ford pickup rust-red and dented, as if it had lost every fight it ever started. It skidded to a stop up ahead, kicking up dust across the road. Doors flew open, and six Trinity Bend boys piled out, big as barns and twice as thick-headed, shoulders straining the seams of their work shirts.

Jesse spat in the dirt. "Well, hell. Look what the cat dragged in."

I knew them on sight. Another chapter, always itching to prove they were harder than us. Brock Rudd led the pack, thick-necked and grinning like a wolf that already smelled blood.

"Well, well," he drawled, folding arms thick as fence posts. "If it ain't Ezekiel's crown prince and his yapping little dog."

Jesse stepped forward first, chin high. "Pocket-sized? Boy, I'll fold you like a road map and sit on ya."

The Trinity boys roared. Brock wiped his eyes like it was the funniest thing he'd heard all week. "Listen to Boone running his mouth. Cute."

Then his eyes slid to me, cold and measuring. "Heard your daddy finally cut the leash, Caleb. Let me off the porch last night."

I cracked my knuckles slowly, feeling the scabs from last night pull tight. "Y'all got business," I said, voice flat, "or just out here showing off them dime-store shirts?"

The words hung for a second. Then Brock's grin widened, and he charged.

Gravel exploded under his boots. His fist came high and heavy, easy to read. I ducked inside it, grabbed a fistful of shirts, and used his own weight to pitch him forward. My shoulder drove into his gut; air whooshed out of him like a busted bellows. Two more piled in, one clamping my arm, the other swinging wild for my ribs.

I twisted hard, yanked the first one into the path of the punch. It landed solidly on his buddy's back. He cursed; I swept his legs and dropped him hard. Behind me, Jesse hit another like a wildcat, the two of them tumbling in a tangle of fists and dust.

It was over quickly. Just enough noise, just enough blood to burn off the poison boys like us carried around. My knuckles split open on Brock's jaw; he staggered, blinked, then let out a low, surprised laugh.

"Damn, Whitlock," he said, working his jaw side to side. "Getting stronger every year."

And just like that, the storm passed.

Laughter rolled out rough and genuine, bloody lips, busted knuckles, shirts half torn off our backs, but grinning all the same. Brock slung a heavy arm across my shoulders like we were old pals.

"Tell your daddy we'll see him at the next gathering," he said. "Try not to burn the whole county down 'fore then."

They climbed back into the truck, still chuckling, and roared off in a cloud of red dust.

Jesse wiped blood from his lip and spat pink into the grass. "Hell of a warm-up, huh?"

"Yeah," I said, dragging air into my lungs.

He elbowed me. "C'mon, we'll be late."

We started walking again. Jesse talked about big plans, dumb jokes, and the same old noise. But inside me, something twisted tighter with every step. Last night's fire. This morning's fight. The easy laughter that followed, as none of it mattered.

Guilt and dust and the smell of blood all mixed up together, winding around my ribs like barbed wire pulling tighter. Jesse never saw it. Nobody did.

I wasn't sure how much longer I could keep it hidden.

KLEIN STEEL FACTORY

They said a man's true colors showed brightest at work, and that morning Ezekiel Whitlock strode into Klein Steel, sure the world was finally about to pay him his due.

He crossed the factory yard with his chin high and his boots polished to a spit-shine, shoulders thrown back like he already wore the supervisor's title. The whistle blew shrill and clear; white men, most of them brothers under the hood, lifted hands in greeting or dipped their chins as he passed.

"Morning, Zeke."

"Boss is calling you up today, I reckon."

"Bout time you ran the whole damn place."

Ezekiel drank it in, clapping back and trading grins, easy as a preacher working a revival tent. In this town, fear and admiration were so knotted together that no one bothered trying to pull them apart.

When the foreman jogged over with a clipboard, Ezekiel straightened his shirtfront like he was headed to the governor's mansion.

"Mr. Whitlock, Mr. Klein needs you in the office. Says it's urgent."

Ezekiel's grin widened. He'd been waiting for this.

He climbed the metal stairs to the glass-walled office that overlooked the floor. Mr. Klein stood inside, shuffling papers and avoiding the window as though he could already feel the heat. Ezekiel knocked once and pushed in.

"Klein," he said, voice thick with certainty. "Good news, I take it?"

Klein managed a thin smile. "Come in, Ezekiel. Shut the door."

Ezekiel stepped inside, chest puffed, arms folded. Ready.

"I know you expected the supervisor spot," Klein began, voice low. "You were considered."

Ezekiel's smile held, but something flickered behind his eyes.

"I'm afraid the position's been filled." Ezekiel blinked once, slowly. "By who?"

The door opened again before Klein could answer. A tall Negro man in a crisp button-down stepped in posture straight, eyes steady, the calm kind of confidence that didn't need to announce itself.

"Morning," he said politely, extending a hand.

"I'm—"

"Don't," Ezekiel snapped, recoiling as though the hand carried plague. "Don't you dare put that near me."

The man lowered his hand without flinching. "Name's Jefferson. I'll be your new supervisor. Looking forward to working together."

Ezekiel's laugh came out harsh and hollow. He wheeled on Klein. "This is your choice? After all I've done here?"

"Mr. Jefferson is qualified," Klein said, voice tight but steady. "Educated. Experienced. He's the best man for the job."

The words struck like a match to dry grass. Ezekiel's face twisted into something raw and ugly, the same look he'd worn once when a preacher dared tell him God answered to no man.

"You little Jewish rat," he hissed. "You and your kind think you can spit in my face in my own town? Replace me with this?"

"That's enough, Mr. Whitlock," Klein cut in.

But Ezekiel was already moving, shoving past Jefferson hard enough to rattle the doorframe. Curses spilled from him as he stormed down the stairs and across the floor, men turning to watch the fury rolling off him like heat off molten steel.

He left the building the way a man leaves for war, high on adrenaline, fists clenched, already planning the fight to come.

SCHOOL CAFETERIA

By lunchtime, the scrap with the Trinity Bend boys had faded into the usual cafeteria roar: scraping, trays clattering, the thick smell of mashed potatoes, pinto beans, and fryer grease hanging in the air like fog. Laughter bounced off the cinder-block walls, crude jokes flying faster than the cornbread.

Jesse and I dropped onto the bench with Tommy Jenkins and the rest of the boys from our crowd. A greasy stack of playing cards already sat in the middle of the table.

"Twenty-one?" Jesse asked, sliding in.

"You know it," Tommy said, flicking a card across the scarred metal.

I dealt myself in, letting the slap of cards on the tabletop drown out everything else. The boys whooped and carried on like the world was nothing but sunshine and easy wins. Laughing along was simpler than thinking, so I did.

Jesse slammed down a blackjack and shot both arms up as if he'd just won the state fair. "Bow down, peasants!"

"The only thing you're winning is a big-mouth contest," I fired back.

The table exploded. Somebody snorted milk out of his nose.

Then the noise shifted, like a cloud sliding over the sun. Heads turned. Conversation dipped. I looked up and saw why.

Mary Beth Hollander was weaving straight toward us, blond curls bouncing, pink lipstick bright as a new dime, wearing a sundress that hugged her curves just enough to make every boy in the room sit taller. She stopped at our table and leaned in, palms on the edge like she owned the place and everybody in it.

"Caleb Whitlock," she said, voice sweet as Coca-Cola, lashes fluttering. "You walking me home after school today?"

A week ago, I might've stammered like a fool. Today, something inside me stayed still and cold.

"Thanks," I said, flat as the tabletop, "but no."

Her smile flickered, just for a heartbeat. She tucked a curl behind her ear. "Are you busy or something?"

"Something like that."

Jesse's jaw hit the table so hard I half expected it to leave a dent. He leaned in, stage-whispering loud enough for the next county to hear: "Caleb, what in the hell?" Then louder, for the whole table: "Boy just turned down Mary Beth Hollander! Do you even like girls?"

The bench erupted in howls, elbows, and somebody pounding the table so hard that a tray jumped. One of the boys choked on cornbread and had to be thumped on the back. I flipped Jesse the bird without looking up. "Shut it."

He wheezed with laughter. "I'm serious, man! You're acting like she ain't the prettiest thing in this school."

"She's just not my type," I said.

The table went quiet for a second, the kind of quiet that waits for a punch line.

Tommy leaned in, eyes narrow and grinning. "All right, Whitlock. Then what exactly is your type?"

I stared at the cards fanned in my hand, the Queen of Hearts staring back like she knew something I didn't. Something turned over slowly in my gut, nameless and heavy.

"Don't know yet," I said at last. "But I'll know when I see it."

Jesse smacked my shoulder. "Listen to him. Talkin' like a damn poet."

The boys roared again, louder than before, but I barely heard them. My mind had already drifted out past the cafeteria windows, past the noise and the grease and the easy, hollow things I'd always thought I wanted. Whatever I was looking for, it wasn't here.

CHAPTER FOUR

The last bell clanged like freedom, and we spilled out of school in a noisy knot: Jesse, Tommy, the rest of the boys laughing, shoving, rehashing the morning brawl, and arguing over who owed whom a Nehi soda.

"Let's hit the park," Jesse said, already veering off the main road.

Nobody argued. It was one of those warm spring afternoons that made you feel half-wild, the air thick with honeysuckle and the promise of trouble. We cut through backyards and empty lots, kicking rusted cans and trading insults, until the trees parted and the old iron bridge came into view. A narrow, rusted walkway arched over lazy brown water, right where the colored school path spilled out.

We climbed onto it just as they appeared. A loose cluster of Negro students, books tucked under arms, voices bright with the day's end. Kids our age, mostly, a few younger, all pressed and polished like Sunday morning. The boys around me went stiff, grins sharpening.

"Well, look what we got here," Tommy muttered lowly. "Field trip's over."

Jesse's eyes lit up like firecrackers. "Let's give 'em a proper send-off."

They leaned over the railing, cupping hands to mouths, letting loose a storm of hoots and ugly words sharpened on years of practice and thrown like stones. I stayed back, hands jammed in my pockets, the noise washing over me like dirty water.

And that's when I saw her.

Lily Jefferson.

She stood a little apart from the others, sunlight pouring over her like it had chosen her special. Skin deep and rich as polished chestnut, tight curls pinned back with a plain barrette that caught the light and threw it back. Her dress was made of blue cotton, with a crisp white collar, but she wore it straight-backed and proud, like armor that fit perfectly.

She wasn't just pretty. She was alive in a way that made everything else fade: fierce, steady, untouchable. The other kids moved around her like planets around a brighter sun.

Jesse bellowed something filthy. The boys howled, stomping boots on the metal grating.

Lily stopped.

She didn't shrink. Didn't hurry. She turned slowly, looked up at the pack of us with eyes dark and bright as new coal, and shook her head slowly, disappointed, like she'd seen this same sorry show a thousand times and still couldn't believe how tired it was.

Then she raised one hand, middle finger high and unflinching.

The bridge exploded with rage and laughter, boys slapping the rail like apes. But Lily was already done with them. Her gaze slid past the noise and landed square on me.

She saw it right away. I wasn't laughing. I wasn't shouting. Wasn't part of it.

For one heartbeat, the world went quiet. Just her eyes on mine, sharp and searching, like she was looking straight through the mask I'd worn my whole life. Something passed between us, electric, impossible, dangerous. A second stretched long enough to change everything.

Then she turned away, curls bouncing, blue dress swaying easily as she walked on down the path with her friends.

Jesse elbowed me hard in the ribs. "Hey! Earth to Caleb—you fall asleep standing up?"

I blinked, dragged my eyes from her disappearing figure. "Yeah," I muttered. "Just tired."

Lie.

In that single, forbidden glance, something inside me had shifted forever.

And I already knew I'd never shift it back.

We cut deeper into the woods behind the park, to our spot where the pines crowded close and the ground stayed damp year-round. Somebody had lined tin cans along a fallen log and hung a couple of rusted license plates from low branches, swaying like lazy wind chimes. The air was thick with pine sap, wet earth, and that sharp, reckless smell boys carry when they think nobody's watching.

Jesse pressed the .22 into my hands first.

"All right, sharpshooter," he grinned. "Try not to shoot your foot off."

I settled the stock against my shoulder, sighted down the barrel, and squeezed.

Ping. Ping. Ping.

Cans jumped and spun into the leaves. Plates rang clean.

"Damn, Caleb!" Tommy whooped. "You could have been a sniper in Korea!"

"Born with a rifle in his crib," Jesse bragged, clapping my back. "Like father, like son."

The words landed wrong, heavy as wet rope. I forced a half-smile and handed the gun over. Like father, like son. The phrase echoed in my head, sour and close, because last night I'd stood at his side while a house burned and children screamed. Last night I'd become something I wasn't sure I could wash off.

We kept shooting and laughing, daring each other to hit farther, trickier shots. For a few minutes, the crack of the rifle and the easy jeering almost drowned everything else out. Almost.

Then an engine growled through the trees, rough and familiar. Jesse shaded his eyes. "Ain't that your daddy's Ford?"

My stomach dropped clean through the ground. There it was, black, dusty, pulled crooked onto the dirt track. The door creaked open, and Ezekiel staggered out, one hand braced on the roof, the other wrapped around a half-empty bottle. Even from here, I could see the sway in his shoulders, the red in his eyes. Drunk before supper. Drunk and mean.

Jesse whistled low. "Something sure lit his fuse."

"Yeah," I muttered. "Reckon I'll catch it later."

The boys watched a moment longer, then shrugged and turned back to the targets like it was nothing. Just Ezekiel being Ezekiel. Normal. I tried to do the same, but the sight of him glaring at empty air, muttering curses we couldn't hear, lodged behind my ribs like a burr.

Jesse took the rifle next, popping off shots and missing half because he couldn't stop laughing at his own jokes. I watched the cans spin and fall, but I wasn't seeing them.

I kept seeing Lily on that bridge, sunlight on her skin, the steady fire in her eyes when she looked straight at me and didn't look away. I kept hearing the screams from last night, thin and high, threading through the smoke. I kept feeling the weight of the bottle in my hand. The moment I crossed a line, I couldn't see my way back over.

Something restless clawed under my skin, hot and urgent. Before I could think better of it, the words slipped out, casual as reloading.

"Y'all ever think about... being with a colored girl?"

The woods went still for half a heartbeat. Then the boys exploded. Tommy doubled over, wheezing. Jesse slapped his knee so hard the rifle barrel dipped.

"Caleb!" Jesse crowed. "What kinda filthy dreams are you having, man?"

"Boy's lost his damn mind," Tommy gasped. "Next he'll wanna marry one!"

They piled on, crude jokes tumbling over each other, the same ugly talk we'd always traded like baseball cards. Jesse straightened, face serious in that proud, preacher way he got sometimes.

"Any white man messing with a colored girl's a race traitor, plain and simple," he declared, like he was reading straight from some invisible book. "Damn right," Tommy echoed.

I nodded. Smiled. Laughed when they looked at me.

"Yeah," I said, voice easy.

But inside, I was somewhere else entirely.

I was back on that bridge, staring into dark, unflinching eyes that saw me, really caught me, and didn't turn away. For the first time I could remember, the man everybody expected me to become felt too small, like a coat I'd outgrown but was still being forced to wear.

And for the first time, I wasn't sure I wanted to keep wearing it.

SUPPER TIME AT WHITLOCK'S. DINNER TABLE.

Supper at our house started quietly enough. The clink of forks on chipped plates, the old wall clock ticking like it was counting down to something, and Daddy's breathing, thick and uneven from the bourbon he'd been drinking since noon. He'd sobered some by the time we sat down, but not near enough. His cheeks still glowed red, and his eyes had that wet, far-off shine I knew too well.

Mama passed the mashed potatoes without a word. I kept my head down, hoping the meal might pass peacefully for once.

It didn't.

Halfway through, Daddy's fork hit the table like a gunshot. "Boy," he growled, "you wanna know what kinda day I had?"

I didn't. But I nodded anyway.

"That damn Jefferson," he spat, the name sour in his mouth. "A colored man, my boss now, telling me how to run my line. Can you believe that?"

I forced my face into something like a scowl, but inside... nothing. No fire, no outrage. Just a hollow confusion, like listening to somebody rage about the sky being the wrong shade of blue. Why did it matter?

"Ain't right," he went on, voice rising. "Ain't natural. White men are born to lead, not take orders from them."

"Yeah," I mumbled, poking at my potatoes.

Mama tried her usual rescue. "So, Caleb," she said, bright and careful, "we heard Mary Beth Hollander came by the table today. Pretty girl. Sweet as they come."

Daddy's mood flipped like a switch. He grinned widely, elbowing me hard enough to rock my chair. "That's my boy. Knew she'd come sniffing around sooner or later. Good blood, that Hollander girl. Fine family. You'll do right by her."

My stomach knotted. I swallowed once, hard. "I turned her down."

The room went dead still. Even the clock seemed to pause.

Daddy blinked. Once. Twice. "You what?"

"I said no," I answered, quieter. "She's not my type."

He stared at me as if I'd just spat on the flag. "Not your type?" he barked. "She's a good white girl, Caleb. Solid stock. Better looking than most in this county. What the hell's wrong with you?"

I shrugged, trying to keep my voice steady. "Just wasn't feeling it."

He let out a mean, barking laugh and waved a hand toward Mama. "Hell, your mama wasn't exactly my type, either, when we started. But a man thinks practically. Bloodlines. Appearances. Keeping what's ours pure."

Mama's fork froze halfway to her mouth. Her smile went stiff, then vanished. She never fought back. Never said a word. I just sat there, taking it, as always.

Daddy leaned in, eyes narrowing, voice dropping low and dangerous. "You listen closely, boy. One day, you'll settle down, and it'll be with a proper white girl. That's how we hold the line. That's how we keep what God and history gave us."

I nodded, the only safe answer. He grunted, satisfied, and went back to his plate, muttering under his breath about the world going soft.

But I wasn't listening anymore.

Across the table, Mama's hands trembled as she passed the cornbread she didn't want. Daddy chewed loudly, already half-gone to whatever came next in his bottle.

And I was back on that bridge.

Lily Jefferson in her blue dress, head high, eyes steady. The way she'd looked at the shouting, laughing boys like they were nothing but noise. The way she'd looked at me as she saw straight through the act I'd been playing my whole life.

Something stirred inside my chest, small but fierce, bright as a coal just catching. I didn't have a name for it yet.

But it was burning, and I had a feeling it wasn't going out anytime soon.

CHAPTER FIVE

The next afternoon hung heavy and thick, the kind of Southern heat that pressed down on you like a wet blanket and made even the cicadas drone lazy and worn out. We cut across the park on the way home, boots kicking up dust from the dry grass, the sun slanting low and gold through the oaks.

Jesse stretched his arms overhead and let out a theatrical yawn.

"Lord, I'm starving. Y'all wanna hit Harrison's? I could put away three cheeseburgers and a mountain of fries."

The boys hollered their yeses, already shoving each other and arguing over who was buying the first round of Cokes. I hung a step or two behind, hands in my pockets, feeling the weight of what I was about to do settle in my chest.

Jesse glanced back. "You coming, Caleb?"

I shook my head quickly, like it was nothing. "Nah. Told Mama I'd head straight home. Chores and such."

It was a thin lie. Mama hadn't said a word about chores, but nobody pressed. They never did. Jesse just shrugged, grinned, and they veered off toward Main Street, voices fading into laughter and horseplay.

The second they were gone, I let out a breath I hadn't realized I'd been holding. My heart started up a hard, steady drum. I'd planned this; I timed it just like yesterday.

I slipped around to the far side of the park, keeping to the shade of the big pecans until the old iron bridge came into view. That was the spot where the colored school let out, where the path narrowed, and the river ran slow and brown below.

I found a place half-hidden by a clump of yaupon and waited; palms damp against my jeans. The minutes dragged, thick as molasses. I told myself I was just curious. I told myself it didn't mean anything. Told myself a lot of things that felt like lies the moment they crossed my mind.

Then she appeared.

Lily Jefferson walked alone today, books hugged to her chest, sky-blue dress catching the late light the same way it had yesterday. She moved easily, head high, like the heat and the weight of the world didn't dare slow her down.

My mouth went dry. Every careful reason I'd given myself scattered like chaff in the wind.

I stepped out from the trees before I could talk myself out of it again.

"Hey," I said, voice rougher than I meant. I lifted one hand in a half-wave, trying to look anywhere but too eager. "Mind if I... walk with you a minute?"

She stopped. Looked me over slowly, eyes sharp and unflinching. For a second, I thought she'd keep walking, figured she'd give me the same single finger salute she'd given the whole bridge yesterday and leave me standing there like the fool I probably was.

Instead, she tilted her head just a fraction. "You got a name, mystery boy?"

"Caleb," I said. "Caleb Whitlock."

Something flickered across her face recognition, maybe caution, but it passed quickly. She started walking again, slow enough that I could fall in beside her.

"Well, Caleb Whitlock," she said, voice low and steady, carrying a smile I couldn't quite see, "you got about five minutes before my daddy starts wondering where I am. Better make 'em count."

I fell into step beside her, careful to keep a respectful distance, hands shoved deep in my pockets so I wouldn't do something stupid like reach for hers.

"Fair enough," I said. "I'll try not to waste 'em."

She glanced over, one eyebrow raised. "Start with why you're really here. And don't give me that 'just to apologize' line."

I let out a short laugh, surprised at how easy it felt. "All right. Truth? I haven't been able to get you outta my head since yesterday. The way you looked up at that bridge full of idiots like you wasn't scared, just... tired of the same old nonsense. And then you looked at me differently. As you saw, I wasn't laughing with 'em."

She didn't say anything right away, just kept walking, but I caught the way her mouth softened.

"I noticed," she said quietly. "You were the only one who didn't open his mouth."

"I wanted to say something," I admitted. "Should've. Didn't. That's part of why I'm here, because I don't want to keep standing quiet when I know it's wrong."

She stopped under the shade of a big pecan tree and turned to face me fully.

"That's easy to say when it's just us talking, harder when your friends are right there. Or your family."

Her words hit like a stone in still water. I nodded slowly. "I know. My daddy... he's Ezekiel Whitlock."

I watched it land. Her eyes widened just a fraction, then narrowed, wary, measuring.

"I figured that might be you," she said, voice lower now. "Everybody knows the name."

"Yeah." I met her gaze steadily. "And I'm telling you because I don't want it hanging between us like some secret. I'm not proud of what he is, what he does. And I don't want to be that."

She searched my face for a long moment, like she was trying to see clear down to the bone.

"That's a hard thing to walk away from," she said finally. "Most don't even try."

"I'm trying," I said. "I don't know how good I'm doing yet. But talking to you... It feels like the first thing that's made sense in a long time."

A small smile tugged at her mouth, real this time, warm and careful.

"You're full of surprises, Caleb Whitlock."

"Good ones, I hope."

She started walking again, her pace now slower. "Maybe. We'll see."

The path curved toward her neighborhood, with modest houses set back from the road, kids' bikes in the yards, and laundry flapping on the lines. The sun was dipping low, turning everything a golden hue.

"So," she said, glancing sideways, "what else you got in those five minutes?"

I grinned, feeling bolder. "Well, I could tell you Jesse once tried to act tough in front of a girl and tripped over his own boots so bad he face-planted in the dirt."

She laughed briefly at first, then more fully, the sound bright and honest. "I would've paid good money to see that."

"Worth every penny," I said. "He still swears the ground jumped up at him."

She shook her head, still smiling. "You're not like I expected."

"Same goes for you."

We walked on, the quiet between us easy now. When her house came into view, green with white trim, curtains moving in the open windows, she slowed.

"That's me," she said, nodding toward it.

I spotted Mr. Jefferson at the kitchen window, dish towel in hand, watching steadily. My stomach tightened.

"Your daddy doesn't miss much," I said.

"He's got a reason," she replied, with no apology in it.

We stopped at the start of her walk. She turned to me, books hugged to her chest.

"Thanks for walking me," she said. "Didn't think I'd end up glad to see one of y'all from that bridge."

"Me neither," I said. "Any chance I could... see you again? Maybe the movies tomorrow night?"

She looked at me for a long moment, something soft and brave in her eyes.

"Yeah," she said. "I'd like that."

My heart jumped out of my chest. "Corner after seven?"

She nodded. "Don't be late."

Then, quick as a heartbeat, she leaned in and brushed a kiss against my cheek, warm, soft, gone before I could do more than breathe.

"Don't let that go to your head," she warned, cheeks flushed, but her smile gave her away.

"Too late," I said, grinning like a fool.

She laughed once more, quietly, and headed up the walk. At the door, she glanced back, just once, like she couldn't help it.

I stood there long after she'd gone inside, cheek still burning, the whole world feeling wider and brighter than it ever had before.

For the first time, I wasn't afraid of where this path might lead.

THE JEFFERSONS' DINNER TABLE

The Jefferson house glowed with warm yellow light as dusk settled over the neighborhood. Inside, the dinner table was set with fried chicken, mashed potatoes, green beans, and a basket of warm biscuits that filled the air with their comforting smell. A slow Sam Cooke song drifted softly from the radio in the corner.

Ruth Jefferson moved around the kitchen, setting down the last bowl. "Dinner's ready," she called, her smile pulling everyone together.

Lily slipped into her seat beside her little brother Isaiah, who squirmed with excitement. Mr. Jefferson took his place at the head of the table, straight-backed but gentle after a long day at the factory.

They bowed their heads and said grace, hands linked, voices low and familiar. Halfway through the meal, Mr. Jefferson looked over at Lily with a raised brow, curious and a touch wary.

"So," he said, cutting into his chicken, "who was that boy walking you home today?"

Lily's fork paused. She felt her mother glance up and Isaiah perk as if he'd just heard gossip. "Just somebody from school," she said carefully.

"A white somebody from school," her father corrected, voice calm but pointed.

Lily sighed. She knew better than to try to dodge him. "His name's Caleb."

She watched her father wait, face unreadable. "Caleb Whitlock," she added quietly.

The room went still. Even the radio seemed quieter.

Mr. Jefferson's knife stopped mid-cut. His jaw tightened. For a long moment, nobody spoke, not even Isaiah. Then he set his utensils down slowly and deliberately.

"Lily," he said, low and steady, "baby, you've got to be careful."

"I know, Daddy."

"No." He leaned forward a little, eyes full of worry. "I don't think you do. It's dangerous, truly dangerous, for a colored girl to be seen with a white boy around here. And if that boy is a Whitlock... Lord, child."

Lily swallowed. "Caleb's not like his daddy."

"I ain't saying he is," her father replied. "But Ezekiel Whitlock is still his daddy. And men like him don't need much excuse to hurt folks."

Ruth reached over and squeezed Lily's hand. "Your daddy's just worried about you, sugar."

"I know," Lily said again, softer this time.

The heaviness hung a moment longer, then Mr. Jefferson let out a slow breath and turned to Isaiah.

"So, son, how was school today?"

Isaiah lit up like a firecracker. "Daddy! I learned how to add really well! And I read a whole book all by myself!"

Mr. Jefferson's face softened into a proud smile. "Did you know? What book?"

"The Cat in the Hat by Dr. Seuss!" Isaiah announced, chest puffed out.

Ruth leaned in with mock surprise. "The whole thing? No skipping pages?"

"No, ma'am!" Isaiah declared, smacking the table for emphasis. "Not even one!"

Everybody laughed, Lily loudest of all. Mr. Jefferson ruffled Isaiah's hair. "Well, look at that. We got ourselves a little scholar."

Isaiah beamed, soaking it in.

The warmth crept back into the room. Biscuits got passed, stories from the day spilled out, and they settled into the easy rhythm of family. But now and then, Mr. Jefferson's eyes drifted to Lily, quiet with questions he hadn't asked yet, and the fear any black father carried in 1950s Texas.

Lily met his gaze once and gave him a small, reassuring smile. She'd be careful. She promised herself she would. But deep down, her heart already knew she couldn't stay away from Caleb Whitlock.

JESSE POV: HARRISON'S DINER

The neon sign at Harrison's Diner buzzed and flickered as evening settled in, spilling a red glow across the cracked sidewalk. Inside, the place thrummed with life. Glasses clinked, the jukebox spun a lively Elvis tune, and the air hung heavy with the smell of fried onions, burgers, and thick milkshakes.

Jesse Boone held court in the center booth, boots propped on the seat, laughing so hard he nearly shot soda through his nose. Clay, Dawson, Mack, and Billy Ray crowded around him, just as loud and rowdy as always.

"Man, I'm telling you," Jesse said, slamming his palm on the table, "Caleb's face when that girl tripped in the gym? It looked like he'd seen a ghost."

The boys roared again. Clay wiped his eyes. "Caleb's been acting strange lately. Never can tell what's going on in that head of his."

"Probably nothing," Billy Ray put in. "He just stares off like he's trying to figure out long division."

"That boy don't think that hard," Mack added, and the table shook with fresh laughter.

Then Mary Beth Hollander appeared, blond curls perfect, pink skirt swishing with every confident step. Every boy sat a little straighter, except Jesse, who leaned back with a lazy, wolfish grin.

"Well, look who showed up," he drawled. "Miss Texas County in the flesh."

Mary Beth smirked. "Hush your mouth, Jesse Boone."

The boys scooted over so she could perch on the edge of the booth. She scanned the diner instead of looking at them. She asked, "Where's Caleb?"

Billy Ray snorted. "Why? You fixing to flirt some more?"

She ignored him. "He doesn't usually miss supper here."

Jesse took a slow sip of his soda. "Caleb's been off tonight. Said he had somewhere to be. Wouldn't say where."

Mary Beth crossed her arms. "Probably dodging me."

Jesse's grin sharpened. "The way he tells it, you ain't exactly his type."

The table exploded again. Clay slapped the counter, and Mack nearly choked on a fry.

Mary Beth's cheeks went pink. "Please. Caleb Whitlock likes me fine. He doesn't wanna say it in front of y'all."

Jesse raised an eyebrow. "If he does, it's news to him."

Mary Beth tossed her hair. "Maybe he just needs me to spell it out clearer."

She tried for confidence, but Jesse caught the uncertainty underneath. He leaned in, voice lower. "Trust me, his mind ain't on you tonight. Something else has got him all twisted up."

She frowned. "Like what?"

Jesse shrugged. "Don't know. But he's quiet. Thinking too much."

"That boy and thinking don't usually go together," Mack joked.

"No," Jesse said, serious now, "this is different."

The laughter died for a moment until the waitress slid a plate of burgers onto the table, and the noise picked right back up. Jesse joined in, popping a fry into his mouth, but his eyes kept drifting to the window and the darkening sky outside.

He and Caleb had been like brothers since they were knee-high. Fought together, got in trouble together, shared everything. Tonight, though, something felt off. Like Caleb was pulling away, slipping out of reach.

Jesse shook it off and laughed at the next joke. But the unease lingered, quiet and stubborn.

"Hey, look." Tommy's voice cut through the chatter. He nodded toward the window.

Across the street, under the orange haze of the streetlights, Caleb walked alone. He was coming from the wrong direction, the side of town everybody knew to steer clear of after dark.

Jesse's stomach tightened.

"What the hell," Tommy muttered. "That's the road to the colored neighborhood?"

The boys craned their necks, whispering. Jesse forced a chuckle. "Probably just running some errand for his daddy. Scouting or something."

They nodded, happy with the easy answer. It fits their worldview.

But Jesse kept watching. Caleb moved with a loose, easy stride, almost light on his feet, like he carried good news instead of trouble. Jesse's excuses crumbled one by one.

What were you doing over there, Caleb? And why didn't you tell me? For the first time, a cold flicker of fear stirred in Jesse's gut. Not for Caleb's safety, but for what it meant if his best friend had started thinking for himself.

CHAPTER SIX

The factory floor thundered with the grind of presses and the sharp bite of metal dust in the air. Men shouted over the clamor, shirts dark with sweat and oil.

Ezekiel Whitlock stood rigid at his station when footsteps approached from behind.

"Whitlock." Mr. Jefferson's voice was calm and professional, and the clipboard was under one arm. "You mixed up the inventory sheets. Take these corrected ones to shipping. Make sure they log them right this time."

Ezekiel turned slowly, eye twitching. "That ain't my—"

"It is now," Jefferson cut in. "And you'll do it."

Silence stretched, broken only by the machines. Ezekiel ground out, "Yes, sir."

Jefferson stepped closer, voice low. "I don't care what you do after hours or what meetings you attend. That's your business. But on my clock, I'm your supervisor. Show respect."

Ezekiel forced the words through clenched teeth. "I understand, sir."

Jefferson nodded once and walked away, boots steady on the concrete. The moment he was gone, Ezekiel's face contorted with fury. He stormed over to a knot of Klan friends near the loading pallets.

"You believe that uppity bastard?" he hissed. "Does he think he can order me around? "His friends muttered in agreement, stoking the rage.

Across the floor, Jefferson knocked on the frosted glass of Mr. Klein's office and stepped inside. Klein looked up from a cluttered desk.

"Production's strong," Jefferson said, closing the door, "but we'll need an extra shift next week."

Klein nodded, scribbling a note. Jefferson hesitated, then added, "There's something else. You know anything about Ezekiel's boy, Caleb?"

Klein set his pen down. "Why?"

"He's been seeing my daughter." Klein leaned back, exhaling slowly. "That'll stir up trouble."

"I know." Jefferson rubbed his forehead. "Just wondering what kind of boy he is."

Klein scratched his chin. "Ezekiel's been grooming him to take over one day. But Caleb's different. Always has been. Polite. Doesn't carry that same hate his daddy does. Never did."

Jefferson nodded, thoughtful. "So you don't think it's some game?"

"If he's sweet on your girl, I'd say no. He ain't like the rest." Klein's eyes narrowed. "But if Ezekiel finds out, all hell breaks loose."

"That's what worries me." Said Mr. Jefferson.

Jesse POV: Madison County High School

Madison County High buzzed with the usual morning chaos. Lockers slammed like gunshots, boys hollered down the corridor, and teachers barked reminders that nobody heeded. Jesse Boone wove through the crowd, spotting Caleb leaning against his locker like he was holding the wall up instead of the other way around.

Caleb looked rough. Hair still wet from a hurried shower, shirt wrinkled as if he'd slept in it. His eyes carried a strange light, too calm, too bright, like he was lit from the inside by something Jesse couldn't name.

Jesse slid up beside him, forcing his usual grin. "Morning, brother."

"Hey," Caleb answered, short and flat.

Jesse studied him longer than he meant to. Something was off. Caleb never looked this awake and this tired at the same time.

"So," Jesse said, keeping it light, "what'd you get up to last night?"

He watched Caleb's face closely. A flicker crossed it, quick as heat lightning, then vanished behind a shrug.

"Nothing much. Stayed home. Homework. Supper. Same old."

Jesse didn't smile. Didn't laugh. He just held Caleb's gaze, searching for the lie he could feel hanging in the air between them. It was only a second or two, but it stretched long enough to make his skin crawl.

Then he clapped Caleb on the back, hard enough to sound friendly. "Yeah. Sure."

The words came out easily, but they tasted wrong. Too careful. Too measured.

Caleb shifted, uneasy. "What's with you?"

"Nothing," Jesse said, shrugging like it was nothing. "Just tired. Come on, bell's fixing to ring."

They started down the hallway side by side, boots echoing on the scuffed tile. Around them, the usual noise rolled on: jokes, shoves, laughter. But between Jesse and Caleb, it felt different now, thinner.

Jesse's grin stayed plastered on, but inside something cold had started to coil. Caleb was holding something back. Jesse could taste it. And whatever it was, it had put the first real crack in the thing they'd always called brotherhood.

He didn't know why it scared him so much.

But it did.

WHITLOCK HOUSE

Later that night, I stood in front of my bedroom mirror, dragging the comb through my hair for the third time. I hadn't gone all out, just a clean button-down and my best jeans, but it still felt wrong, like I was dressing for a life that didn't belong to my father. A better one, maybe. One I could choose.

I tucked in the shirt, drew a deep breath, and headed downstairs. Daddy stepped out of the living room the second my foot hit the bottom step, coffee mug in hand, eyes narrowed the way they always got when he smelled something he didn't like.

"Where are you off to, looking that sharp?" he asked, eyebrow climbing. "Ain't like you to fuss on a Monday night."

I shrugged, trying to keep it light. "Just meeting somebody."

He crossed his arms. "Who?"

I forced the name out before I could think better of it. "Mary Beth Hollander."

His face lit up as I'd just told him I'd been made a grand wizard. Pride rolled off him so thick it turned my stomach.

"That's my boy," he said, clapping my shoulder hard enough to jolt me. "Good stock, that Hollander girl. Pure. Comes from the right kind of people."

I managed a tight smile. He stepped aside, reached for the keys on the mantel, and dangled them in front of me.

"Take the Ford. Show her what a Whitlock looks like when he means business."

I stared at the keys, stunned. "Really?"

"Don't make me regret it," he said, but his grin said he already felt like father of the year.

"Thank you, sir."

I took the keys and got out of there before he could change his mind or ask more questions. The evening air hit me cool and clean, carrying the dust and cut grass, as well as the faint tang of motor oil. I unlocked the Ford, slid behind the wheel, and felt my pulse kick up, not from nerves about lying, but from the thrill of what came next.

Tonight wasn't about Mary Beth or Daddy's plans or any of it.

Tonight was about Lily.

I turned the key. The engine rumbled to life. I eased down the driveway and onto the road toward town, windows down, warm wind whipping through the cab.

I never saw the headlights flick on behind the hedges. Never noticed the old Chevy pickup pull out slowly and quietly.

Jesse Boone sat hunched over the wheel, jaw tight, eyes fixed on my taillights. He kept his distance, three car lengths back, tucked in the growing shadows.

I didn't know he was there.

But he wasn't letting me out of his sight tonight. Not until he knew exactly where I was going and who I was going to see.

CHAPTER SEVEN

I eased the Ford to the curb in front of Lily's house, palms slick against the steering wheel. The porch light spilled warm gold over the steps. Then she stepped out, wearing a soft blue dress that caught the light just right. My chest tightened so hard I forgot to breathe for a second.

She smiled, a small, nervous, yet genuine smile. "You clean up nice, Caleb Whitlock."

"You look beautiful," I said, and the words came out rough with truth.

She blushed, climbed in beside me, and pulled the door shut. As I eased away from the curb, she kept stealing little glances my way, like she needed to make sure I hadn't vanished.

We drove to the only theater in town, the one split down the middle: white seats downstairs, colored seats in the balcony. My knuckles went white on the wheel when we pulled into the lot.

Lily noticed. She reached over and touched my arm. "It's okay," she whispered. "Up top's better anyway. Quieter."

Inside, nobody looked twice. She led the way up the narrow stairs to the balcony, and we slipped into the back row. My heart hammered louder than the projector whirring behind us.

The lights dimmed. The picture started. After a few minutes, Lily leaned closer, her shoulder brushing mine. Her hand settled on the armrest between us. I stared at it a second, then slid my fingers over hers. She turned her palm up and laced them tight. In the glow from the screen, her smile lit the dark better than any movie ever could.

The picture on the screen turned soft and romantic: moonlight, a garden, two lovers meeting slowly. The music played gently.

Lily looked over at me. I looked at her. She leaned in first. I met her halfway.

Her lips were warm, soft, and careful. But the kiss struck me like lightning straight to the heart. Everything I'd never known I needed poured into me all at once. The theater, the town, the rules, my father's voice, all of it vanished. There was only her.

Jesse POV: Movie theater

Downstairs in the white section, Jesse Boone moved quietly through the aisle, collar turned up, old baseball cap pulled low. He took a seat on the far left, close enough to the balcony stairs to glance upward without drawing eyes.

He scanned the shadows above until he found them.

Caleb and Lily Jefferson. Side by side. Her head rested easily on his shoulder. Their hands locked together like it was the most natural thing in the world.

Jesse went still. The air left his lungs in a slow, painful leak. His stomach twisted hard. Caleb? His Caleb? The boy who'd grown up beside him, sworn the same oaths, carried the same blood? The one everybody said would step into Ezekiel's shoes one day?

His jaw locked so tight his teeth ached. Disbelief burned behind his eyes, hot and sharp.

Jesse watched them kiss and felt something inside him crack clean open.

His hands curled into fists on his knees. Breathing came shallow. Confusion and hurt tangled with a rising, helpless anger. Caleb had lied and hidden this from him, choosing her instead.

He sat frozen in the dark, eyes fixed on the balcony, shaking with the weight of it.

His best friend, his brother in everything but blood, was turning his back on everything they'd been raised to hold sacred.

And Jesse knew, with a cold, sinking certainty, that he couldn't let this go.

Not anymore.

Ezekiel's House

Jesse Boone drove straight to the Whitlock place, anger churning hot in his chest. He barely parked before jumping out and bounding up the porch steps.

Ezekiel opened the door, beer bottle in hand. "Jesse? What brought you here this late?"

Jesse swallowed hard. "Sir... I need to tell you something. About Caleb."

Ezekiel's face turned to stone. "Come inside."

Minutes later, Jesse finished. The theater. The balcony. The kiss. Every word tasted like betrayal.

Ezekiel said nothing for a long, heavy moment. Then a cold smile spread across his face.

"Thank you, Jesse."

CALEB POV:

Driving Lily home felt like floating on air. She sat close, humming softly under her breath, the glow from the movie still clinging to her. Every time I stole a glance, she smiled like she carried a secret made of pure light. When I pulled up to her house, neither of us moved right away. Crickets filled the night. The porch lamp cast a gentle gold over everything.

"I had a real good time tonight," I said, voice low.

"Me too," she whispered, eyes shining.

She leaned in, hands sliding up to the back of my neck. Her lips found mine again, deeper this time, slower, full of something that set fire racing through my veins. I pulled her closer by the waist, lost in her completely.

When we finally broke apart, we were both breathless.

"I'll see you soon," she said, thumb brushing my cheek.

I didn't want to let go. She stepped back, gave me one last soft smile, and turned toward the house.

As she reached the porch, the door opened. Mr. Jefferson stood there, arms folded. He had to have seen the kiss. Lily paused, then slipped inside. The door closed quietly behind her.

I sat there a moment longer, dread and hope knotted tight in my gut.

Lily POV: Inside the Jefferson Home

Mr. Jefferson waited until Lily set her purse on the table before he spoke, voice quiet but firm.

"Lily... that boy. That was Caleb Whitlock, wasn't it?"

She hesitated only a heartbeat. "Yes, Daddy."

He rubbed his forehead and let out a slow breath. "I ain't mad. But you need to understand how dangerous this is."

"I know," she said softly. "But he's not like the others."

Mr. Jefferson studied her face, saw the truth shining there, and sighed deeply.

"Then bring him to supper," he said at last.

Lily's eyes widened. "Really?"

"Yes. I want to look him in the eye myself."

She nodded, relief flooding her features. But worry still shadowed his gaze as he turned away.

THE WHITLOCK HOUSE

By the time I eased the Ford into the driveway, I felt lighter than I had in years. I slipped inside quietly, hoping not to wake Mama. I never expected Daddy to be waiting in the hallway shadows.

"Where have you been?" His voice cut low and sharp.

"I—"

He didn't let me finish. His hand shot out, grabbed my shirt, and slammed me against the wall. A picture frame rattled loose and fell to the ground.

"You lying little coward," he snarled, breathing hot with rage. "Think you can pull one over on me? Jesse saw everything."

My heart dropped like a stone. "Dad—"

"Shut your mouth." His fist twisted tighter in the fabric. "You stay away from that girl. You hear me? Stay away, or I'll make you wish you'd never been born."

He shoved me hard one last time and stormed down the hall. I slid down the wall, legs giving out, chest heaving with fear and fury.

From the kitchen came the scrape of the phone off the hook. His voice dropped to a venomous whisper.

"Yeah... It's time. We will move soon."

A pause.

"The Jew's gonna pay for hiring that negro. Let's remind 'em who really runs this town."

Ice flooded my veins. I knew exactly what those words meant.

CHAPTER EIGHT

The next morning, the air hung thick and heavy as I trudged toward school, like the whole town had eyes on me and knew every secret from the night before. My cheek still carried the ghost of Lily's kiss, but the warmth felt distant now, crowded out by a cold knot in my gut.

Jesse waited at the corner, arms folded tight across his chest, face drawn and hard.

"You didn't tell me," he said the second I got close, voice low and edged with something sharp.

I kept walking, boots scuffing the gravel. "Didn't figure it was your business."

He fell beside me, jaw clenched so tight I could see the muscle jump. "Not my business? Caleb, you were out with a colored girl, on a date. That kinda thing can get you killed. Hell, it could get me killed just for standing too close."

I stopped dead and turned to face him. "Her name's Lily. And she ain't just some girl. She's... different."

Jesse grabbed my arm, fingers digging in. "Different? She's—"

"Don't." I yanked free, voice cracking like a whip. "Don't you say that word. Not about her. Not to me."

He stared at me, eyes wide, like I was a stranger wearing his best friend's face. The hurt in them cut deeper than any anger.

"You're throwing everything away," he said finally, voice quieter now. "For her."

"Maybe I'm tired of the things we're supposed to hold on to," I said. "Maybe I'd rather be a fool than keep pretending to be what everybody wants."

Jesse shook his head slowly, the fight draining out of him, leaving only raw pain. He turned and walked ahead without another word. We covered the rest of the way to school in silence, the space between us wider than it had ever been.

THE BRIDGE

After school, I spotted Lily waiting by the old oak tree near the school steps, surrounded by a knot of her friends. When her eyes found mine across the crowd, her face lit up in a way that hushed every noise inside my head.

She said something quickly to the girls and walked over, hands clasped behind her back as if she were trying to play it cool. Her smile betrayed her completely.

"I wasn't sure you'd come talk to me today," she said, voice light but teasing.

"I wouldn't miss it for anything," I replied.

We drifted away from the others, slow and easy, until we reached the shade under the iron bridge where the river ran quietly below. Nobody bothered us here.

She stopped and turned to me, eyes searching mine. "My daddy... he wants you to come for supper. Tomorrow night."

My heart stuttered, a mix of nerves and something brighter. "Really?"

"Really," she said, biting her lip to hide a bigger smile. "He says he needs to see the boy who's been taking up all my time."

I laughed under my breath. "Fair enough. He's got every right."

"So you'll come?" she asked, quieter now, hopeful.

"Yeah," I said, meaning it with everything in me. "I'll be there."

We stood there a moment, words no longer needed. The river murmured below, cicadas buzzed overhead, and the space between us felt charged with something new and fearless.

Then she reached up, fingers curling into the front of my shirt. She tugged me close and kissed me, soft at first, testing, then deeper, warm and specific. I slid my hands to her waist, pulling her in, losing myself in the taste of her and the way she fit against me.

When we finally parted, both of us were breathless and smiling like fools.

She touched my cheek once, quick and tender, then turned toward home.

I watched her go, the sun catching in her curls, and walked the other way with a grin I couldn't wipe off if I tried. For the first time in a long while, tomorrow felt like something worth waking up for.

THE KLEIN'S HOUSE

The night air was thick and still as Daddy slammed the car door, the bang rolling across the empty fields like a warning shot. A dozen hooded figures waited in the shadows, torches already lit, flames dancing hungry and orange.

He grabbed my shoulder hard enough to bruise. "You're coming with us tonight, boy. Time you remembered who you are."

I swallowed the protest burning in my throat. Arguing would only make it worse, especially with Jesse standing a few feet away, eyes fixed on me like he was waiting to see if I'd finally break.

I climbed onto the truck bed with the others. Engines growled to life, and we tore down the back roads, dust and sparks trailing behind us. My stomach twisted tighter with every mile.

We stopped at the edge of Mr. Klein's property, the Jewish factory owner who'd dared hire Mr. Jefferson. The house sat quiet and dark, innocent in the moonlight.

Daddy's voice cut through the night. "Light it."

Two men jammed a wooden cross into the soft front lawn. Gasoline soaked the base, and a match turned it into a roaring pillar of fire. Flames clawed at the sky, painting everything in angry orange.

"Now the window," Daddy said, pressing a heavy rock into my hand. It felt cold and wrong against my palm. I stared at it, my throat closing. Every part of me screamed no.

"Throw it, boy."

His eyes bored into me, hard as iron. Jesse watched too, silent. The others waited.

My fingers shook. I drew back and let the rock fly.

Glass exploded inward with a sharp, violent crash. A woman screamed inside, high and terrified. Mr. Klein's voice roared something furious as he rushed to the broken window, silhouette frantic against the firelight.

The men howled approval, torches waving like victory flags.

Bile rose in my throat. I felt sick, hollowed out, the roar of their laughter ringing in my ears like an accusation.

We rode away, engines snarling, the cross still burning bright behind us. My hands trembled on the truck's side rail. Each flicker of torchlight felt like judgment. Each mile toward home dragged me closer to a line I couldn't keep pretending to stand on.

I had done what they wanted. But inside, something had finally snapped.

Daddy would know soon enough, and when he did, there'd be no going back.

CHAPTER NINE

The next afternoon, after school, I found Lily waiting under the big oak behind the building, her arms wrapped tightly around herself, as if she were holding everything in. The second her eyes met mine, her face hardened, hurt and anger flashing bright.

My stomach dropped straight through the ground.

"Caleb," she said, voice low and steady, "we need to talk."

She knew.

"I heard about Mr. Klein's place last night," she continued, stepping closer. "A cross burned in his yard. Rock through his window. And don't even try to tell me you weren't part of it."

The words hit like punches. I opened my mouth, but nothing came out at first. The air around us felt thick; the old oak looming overhead seemed to be listening.

"Lily... it wasn't what you thought."

Her eyes narrowed. "Then tell me what it was, Caleb. Because from where I'm standing, it looks real clear. Your daddy drags you out on one of his night rides, and the next thing folks hear, the man who hired my father has a burning cross on his lawn."

Her voice cracked on the last few words, and it cut me deeper than any shout could have.

"I didn't want any part of it," I said, the confession spilling out rough and raw. "He made me go. Made me help light the cross. Made me throw that rock. I stood there hating every second, Lily. Hating myself."

She turned away for a moment, jaw tight, staring out toward the river. I braced for her to walk off, to leave me standing there with nothing but the weight of what I'd done.

Instead, she spun back, closing the distance until we were only inches apart. Her eyes blazed, but something softer flickered behind the anger.

"You drive me absolutely crazy," she said, voice trembling just a little. "You do the stupidest things because you're scared of that man. But..."

She let out a long, shaky breath and shook her head.

"...I love you anyway, you dumb fool."

The words broke something open inside me. Relief and shame crashed together so hard I could barely stand. I didn't deserve her forgiveness, not after last night. But hearing it poured through me like sunlight after a storm.

"I'm sorry," I whispered, throat thick. "I'm so damn sorry."

She didn't say anything more. She didn't need to. She reached for me, slow at first, then sure, and I pulled her into my arms. She held on fiercely, cheek pressed to my chest, fingers digging into my back like she was anchoring us both.

I wrapped my arms around her tight, burying my face in her hair, breathing her in. We didn't kiss. We just stood there under the oak, holding each other while the world stayed quiet around us.

After a while, we sank into the cool grass, her head resting against my chest, my arms still around her. My heart finally slowed. For the first time since burning that cross lit up the night, I could breathe.

She wasn't letting go.

And God help me, I wasn't ever letting go of her.

THE JEFFERSON'S HOUSE

I pulled up to the Jefferson house with my stomach in knots, the Ford's engine ticking as it cooled in the quiet evening air. The place looked warm from the outside, with yellow light spilling from the windows and the smell of fried chicken drifting on the breeze. I wiped my palms on my jeans, took a deep breath, and knocked.

Mr. Jefferson opened the door himself. He filled the frame, tall and straight, eyes steady but not unkind. "Caleb," he said, voice even. "Come on in."

I stepped inside, hat in hand. The house smelled of good cooking and polish, everything neat and lived-in. Isaiah peeked around the corner, wide-eyed and curious, while Mrs. Jefferson smiled from the kitchen doorway.

Lily stood near the table, looking beautiful in a simple dress, her smile small but real. It steadied me more than anything else could have.

We sat down to eat. Fried chicken, mashed potatoes, green beans, and cornbread still warm from the oven. Mr. Jefferson said grace, his deep voice filling the room with thanks and quiet strength. I kept my hands folded and my head bowed, feeling the weight of being here, in this house, at this table.

The conversation started carefully. Mrs. Jefferson asked about school. Isaiah chattered about a book he was reading. I answered politely, trying not to let my nerves show.

Then Mr. Jefferson looked straight at me. "So, Caleb. Lily says you're a good student. What do you plan to do after graduation?"

The question hung there, simple on the surface but heavy underneath. I set my fork down.

"I'm not sure yet, sir," I said honestly. "My daddy's got ideas. But I'm trying to figure out my own."

He nodded slowly, studying me. "That's a hard thing. Knowing when to follow and when to choose your own road."

Lily glanced at me, eyes soft with encouragement.

"I'm learning," I said. "It ain't easy."

Mrs. Jefferson smiled gently. "It takes courage even to start."

Isaiah piped up. "You like baseball, Caleb? I got a new glove!"

The tension eased a little. We discussed safer topics, such as games, school, and the weather. But now and then, Mr. Jefferson's eyes came back to me, measuring, not hostile but careful. He was observing the kind of man who sat at his table.

When the plates were cleared, and the pie came out, he leaned back and spoke quietly.

"You treat my daughter right, Caleb. That's all I ask. The world out there's hard enough without adding more hurt."

I met his gaze steadily. "Yes, sir. I aim to."

He nodded once, and something shifted. Not yet full approval, but a start.

Lily walked me to the porch later, the night cool around us. She squeezed my hand.

"You did well," she whispered.

"So did you," I said. "Your family's really nice."

She smiled, leaned in, and kissed me softly and quickly. As I drove home, the knot in my stomach had loosened. For the first time, I felt like maybe, just maybe, there was room in this world for us.

CHAPTER TEN

I pulled up to the Jefferson place earlier than any reasonable person should on a Saturday, my hands still sweaty on the steering wheel. The house looked peaceful in the morning light, with curtains fluttering in the breeze, a thin trail of smoke rising from the chimney, as if they were already cooking breakfast. I sat there a minute, staring at the neat green paint and the flowers Mrs. Jefferson kept along the walk. This was the right thing to do, but my stomach didn't seem to agree.

Before I could climb out and knock, the screen door creaked open. Mr. Jefferson stood there, coat slung over his arm, a small smile tugging at his mouth like he'd been expecting my truck.

"Caleb," he called, voice warm but direct. "Good to see you, son. Got a minute before we eat?"

"Always, sir," I answered, stepping out and shutting the door quieter than I needed to.

He nodded toward his old Chevy. "Hop in. You and I have a little errand to run."

I climbed in beside him, curiosity mixing with the nerves. We didn't talk much on the short drive. Just the low rumble of the engine and the occasional comment about the weather or how the cotton was coming in. When he turned down the familiar road toward Mr. Klein's place, my heart slammed against my ribs.

The house came into view, and there it was: the broken window staring back like an accusation, shards still glittering on the sill in the morning sun. The charred patch on the lawn from the cross had been raked over, but the scar remained.

I couldn't breathe right. "Mr. Jefferson... I don't think I should be here."

"That's exactly why you should," he said, voice gentle but firm. He cut the engine and looked over at me. "You can't undo what's done, son. But you can help make it right. Come on."

He climbed out and went to the truck bed, pulling out a fresh pane of glass, a hammer, nails, a putty knife, and a small bucket. He handed me the hammer and the glass as if it were the most natural thing in the world.

I took them, hands already shaking. "Sir... this is because of me. I threw that rock."

"I know," he said quietly, no judgment in his tone. Just a fact. "And now you're gonna help fix what you broke. That's how a man starts to make amends."

We walked up to the house together. Mr. Klein met us at the door, looking tired but not surprised. He shook Mr. Jefferson's hand, then mine, his grip firm.

"Thank you for coming," he said. No anger. No lecture. Just thanks.

We got to work. Mr. Jefferson showed me how to measure twice, how to carefully pry out the old shards without cutting myself, how to sweep the frame clean, and how to seat the new glass snug and true. My hands fumbled at first, clumsy with guilt and nerves. Every time the hammer slipped or I dropped a nail, I waited for a sharp word.

It never came.

"Easy now," he said instead, steadying my wrist. "Take your time. Good work ain't rushed."

We fitted the glass into place, sealed it with putty, and smoothed the edges to ensure they were neat and even. The sun climbed higher, warming our backs. Sweat beaded on my forehead, but it felt clean, honest.

Halfway through, Mr. Klein brought out glasses of cold lemonade. We sat on the porch steps for a minute, drinking in silence.

"You're a good boy, Caleb," he said finally, eyes on the horizon. "It takes guts to stand here today."

I swallowed hard. "Don't feel like guts, sir. Feels like the least I could do."

Mr. Jefferson nodded beside me. "That's where it starts."

We finished the job. The new window caught the sunlight cleanly and clearly, with no cracks or scars. Mr. Klein shook my hand again, longer this time.

"Thank you," he said, and meant it.

On the drive back, Mr. Jefferson didn't say much until we were almost home.

"You did well today, son."

I stared out the window, throat tight. "I wish you'd been the one raising me," I said before I could stop myself. The words hung there, raw and honest.

He was quiet for a long moment. Then his big hand settled on my shoulder, warm and sure.

"Blood doesn't make a father, Caleb. Heart does. And yours is in the right place. Just keep listening to it."

I nodded, blinking hard against the burn in my eyes. For the first time, somebody saw me as more than Ezekiel Whitlock's son. Saw someone worth guiding, worth believing in.

We pulled up to his house, the smell of breakfast drifting out to meet us. I climbed out feeling lighter, like some of the weight I'd carried had stayed behind in that fresh putty and glass.

Simple work. Honest work.

But it felt like the beginning of something I could finally be proud of.

JESSE POV

Jesse Boone sat with the boys at their usual spot, the rusted-out grain silo behind the Texaco station. The sun hung low over the cotton fields, painting everything in a tired golden light. The others laughed and carried on, passing a warm Coke and trading stories, but Jesse barely heard them.

His eyes kept drifting to the dirt road. No dust clouds. No familiar truck rumbling up.

No Caleb.

Hours slipped by. The laughter faded as the sky darkened, but still no sign. Jesse's jaw tightened until it ached. Something sour and sharp coiled in his gut. Caleb was always here. Always first to show, last to leave. They were brothers in everything that mattered.

But tonight he was off somewhere else with someone else.

Jesse stood suddenly, boots scraping concrete.

"Where are you headed?" Tommy called.

Jesse didn't answer. He climbed into his daddy's old Chevy, fired it up, and drove straight to Whitlock's place. He took the porch steps two at a time and pounded on the door hard enough to rattle the hinges.

Ezekiel opened it, irritation etched deep. "Jesse? What the hell are you doing here this late?"

"I'm looking for Caleb," Jesse said, voice rough. "He never showed at the silo."

Ezekiel's eyes narrowed. "He ain't home yet?"

Jesse shook his head. The memory of the theater balcony burned behind his eyes. Caleb and that Jefferson girl, hands locked, lips meeting. Poison churned in his stomach.

Ezekiel studied him for a long second, then stepped aside. "Get in here."

Jesse crossed the threshold. The door shut heavily behind him, lock clicking like a judge's gavel. Ezekiel led him into the den, poured two fingers of bourbon, and threw half of it back in one swallow.

"That boy..." he growled, voice thick with disgust. "He's a disgrace."

Jesse stayed quiet, throat tight.

Ezekiel set the glass down hard and looked at him, something weary and hateful flickering in his eyes. Then he placed a heavy hand on Jesse's shoulder.

"You know, Jesse, sometimes I swear I wish you were the one I raised. You understand loyalty. Discipline. What it means to stand with your own kind. Caleb... he's always been soft. Weak in the heart."

Jesse's chest swelled, pride and grief tangling together. He nodded, not trusting his voice.

In the kitchen, just beyond the half-closed door, Annabelle Whitlock stood frozen. The mixing bowl in her hands trembled. Silent tears welled in her eyes, but she didn't let them fall. She listened, heart breaking for the son she still believed in.

Ezekiel's voice dropped lower, cold as winter iron.

"If that boy turned his back on his own blood... on everything we stand for... he'll answer for it."

The words hung in the air like smoke, thick and choking.

Jesse swallowed hard, the taste of betrayal bitter on his tongue. He had come looking for his friend.

Instead, he had helped light the fuse.

WHITLOCK HOUSE

That evening, I stepped through the door feeling lighter than I had in years, as some of the weight I'd carried had finally lifted. But Mama was waiting in the hallway. She grabbed my arm and pulled me close, her grip urgent.

"Caleb," she whispered, eyes wide with worry, "where were you?"

I hesitated. "With Lily."

Her face softened, and something tender broke through the fear. She reached up and cupped my cheeks in her hands.

"Do you love her?" she asked, voice gentle as a prayer.

I swallowed hard. "Yes, ma'am. I think I do."

She nodded slowly, like she had known it long before I did.

"Don't hide from that," she said. "Don't let this house or your father steal it from you. I married a man I didn't love because I was afraid of being alone. Don't you be afraid, baby."

"Mama..." My voice cracked.

"I don't want to end up like him," I whispered.

"You won't," she said fiercely, pulling me into a hug. "Your heart ain't made of the same poison."

For a moment, wrapped in her arms, I felt safe. Seen. Loved for who I was, not who I was supposed to be.

Then came the knock at the door, sharp and insistent.

Two of the boys stood on the porch, Tommy and Ray, grinning wide like nothing was wrong.

"Come on, Caleb!" Tommy called. "We're heading to the woods to do some shooting!"

I didn't want to go. Every instinct screamed to stay inside, to hold onto the warmth Mama had just given me. But saying no would raise questions I couldn't answer yet. So I forced a smile and followed.

We piled into the truck, laughing on the way, shoving each other, trading the same old dumb jokes. For a little while, it almost felt normal. The truck stopped just before the clearing in the woods. We got out and walked a few steps.

Then the laughter died.

I turned and realized they had formed a circle around me in the clearing. No rifles. No cans set up for targets. Just hard eyes and silence.

"What're y'all doing?" I asked, trying to keep my voice steady.

Nobody answered. Ray grabbed my arms from behind. Tommy ripped my shirt off in one rough yank. Before I could fight back, they shoved me against a pine and looped coarse rope around my wrists, tying me tight to the trunk.

"Hey!" I shouted, twisting against the burn. "What the hell is this?"

Footsteps crunched through the leaves. Jesse stepped out of the shadows, a bullwhip coiled in his hand. His eyes were red-rimmed and glassy, like he hadn't slept in days. He looked broken.

"I'm sorry, Caleb," he said, voice barely above a whisper.

"But you sinned. And we gotta make it right."

"Jesse, please," I begged, panic rising. "Don't do this."

CRACK.

The first lash cut across my back like liquid fire. I gasped, vision blurring.

CRACK.

The second tore a raw scream from my throat. My knees buckled, but the rope held me up.

Again and again the whip fell. Each strike stole my breath, my strength, my hope.

Through the trees, half-hidden in the darkness, Ezekiel Whitlock stood watching. Arms crossed. A cold, satisfied smile on his face. Pride restored as his son paid in blood for daring to love the wrong girl.

The pain in my back throbbed with every heartbeat, a constant fire that kept me half-awake in the dark. Tied to that tree, blood cooling on my skin, I drifted in and out, too weak to shout anymore. The night sounds blurred together: crickets, wind in the pines, my own ragged breathing.

Then came footsteps. Fast. Desperate.

Mama burst through the brush, coat flapping, face pale in the moonlight. She carried Daddy's old revolver in one hand and a kitchen knife in the other.

"Baby?" Her voice broke as she saw me. "Oh God, Caleb..."

She dropped to her knees, knife flashing as she sawed at the ropes. They gave way, and I collapsed forward into her arms. She caught me, warm and solid, wrapping her coat around my shivering shoulders.

"Who did this?" she whispered, fingers gentle on the torn skin of my back. "Who?"

I could barely speak. "Daddy... Jesse... the others."

Her whole body went rigid. She helped me sit against the tree, eyes searching mine in the dim light.

"I heard him planning it," she said, voice trembling with rage and fear. "After Jesse came by. He was talking about striking first at the Jeffersons. About sending a message they wouldn't forget. Said if you wouldn't learn your lesson one way, he'd make sure the people you cared about paid for it."

The words hit harder than any whip. Lily. Her family.

I pushed myself up, legs shaky but holding. "I have to go to her."

Mama tried to steady me. "Caleb, you're hurt—"

"I have to."

She looked at me for a long moment, then pressed the revolver into my hand. Her fingers lingered on mine, warm and sure.

"Be careful," she whispered. "And come back to me."

I nodded, throat too tight for words. Then I ran.

The woods blurred past, branches whipping my face, pain shooting through my back with every step. But I didn't slow. I couldn't. I pictured them already moving: trucks loaded with men in white sheets, guns across their laps, Daddy in the lead with that cold righteous fire in his eyes. Jesse was riding along, face drawn, telling himself this was justice.

They were going after Lily first. I knew it the way I knew my own name.

The gun felt heavy in my hand, but I held it tight. My breath burned in my lungs, blood pounded in my ears, and the night rushed by in streaks of shadow and moonlight.

I wasn't going to let them reach her.

Not tonight.

Not ever.

CHAPTER ELEVEN

The Jefferson house radiated a cozy golden glow against the chill of the deepening night, the faint strains of upbeat music wafting through the cracked-open windows like a gentle lullaby. Inside the living room, bursts of warm laughter echoed as Lily's little brother awkwardly copied his father's smooth dance moves, his small feet tangling clumsily and sending him into delighted giggles. Lily clapped her hands in glee, her own laughter bubbling up bright and carefree, while Ruth twirled gracefully with her husband, their bodies swaying in perfect harmony born from years of deep, unwavering love.

It was one of those perfect, ordinary evenings, the kind that wrapped their home in an illusion of unbreakable safety, where worries felt distant, and the world outside seemed kind. Ruth paused her dancing, a light sheen of sweat on her forehead, and stepped away with a lingering smile to fetch a glass of water from the kitchen. The cool tile felt refreshing under her bare feet as she approached the sink, still humming softly to the music.

Then she looked up.

Her breath caught in her throat like a trapped scream. There, pressed against the windowpane, was a face unnaturally pale, like bleached bone under a crude hood, with ragged eyeholes staring unblinking into her soul. The figure loomed motionless, its presence a cold violation that turned her blood to ice. A raw, piercing scream tore from Ruth's lungs, shattering the peaceful air as terror flooded every vein. The glass slipped from her numb fingers, exploding into a thousand sharp fragments across the floor, the sound echoing like gunfire in the sudden silence.

Outside, from the thick shadows of the yard, more hooded figures emerged, silent and relentless. Dozens of them, their white robes ghostly in the moonlight, closing in like a noose around the house. The flickering orange glow of their torches cast hellish shadows on the ground, the acrid smell of burning pitch already seeping through the cracks, thick and choking.

"Ruth!" Henry Jefferson burst into the kitchen, his face draining of color as she staggered back, her hands trembling violently. "They're here," she whispered, her voice breaking into a sob of pure dread. "They're surrounding us."

Henry's expression turned to stone, a fierce resolve hardening his features as raw fear clawed at his chest. He yanked open the drawer beneath the counter, his hands steady despite the storm inside, and pulled out the shotgun hidden there. With swift, mechanical precision, he loaded the shells, the metallic clicks loud in the terrified quiet.

"Get the kids to the back bedroom now. Lock the door and stay down," he ordered, his voice low and unnaturally calm, betraying none of the panic roaring in his ears.

Ruth nodded through her tears and bolted from the room, her heart pounding like a war drum. Henry pumped the shotgun with a sharp, ominous rack that filled the house with its deadly promise. He took a position behind the front window, jaw locked tight, muscles coiled as he peered into the night. The Klan had fanned out across the lawn, their torches blazing brighter, rifles glinting coldly in the firelight, faces hidden beneath those hateful hoods.

Then the first shot rang out, a deafening crack that splintered the night and hurled them all into unimaginable horror.

CALEB POV

My lungs were ablaze, each desperate pull of air scraping like broken glass down my raw throat. The night tasted bitter and sharp, thick with the chill that numbed my face but did nothing to dull the agony inside me. I ran harder, legs churning through the emptiness of Main Street, sneakers hammering the pavement so violently the jolt shot up my spine with every stride.

"Please... please let me get there in time," I begged into the dark, the words ripping out between sobs I could no longer hold back. Tears blurred the world into streaks of yellow light and shadow.

The storefronts rushed by in a haze of locked doors and indifferent windows. Streetlamps hummed overhead like furious hornets, their weak glow flickering over the deserted sidewalk, throwing long, mocking shadows that chased me. None of it mattered. Nothing mattered except the distance still stretching ahead, cruel and endless.

My ribs throbbed with a deep, crushing pain that made me want to double over, but I refused to slow. Blood poured from the wounds on my back, hot and slick, soaking my shirt until it clung cold and heavy against my skin. With every frantic step, fresh warmth spilled down my spine, the metallic scent flooding my nose, mixing with the salt of sweat and tears.

Lily. My Lily. The thought of her alone in that house clawed at my heart, tore screams I had no breath left to voice. I gripped the gun so tightly my knuckles ached, the metal slick with sweat and blood.

"Just hold on, baby... please, God, hold on," I pleaded, voice cracking into something small and broken. "I'm coming. I'm coming. Please don't leave me. Please don't leave me."

The words dissolved into ragged sobs as I forced my burning body onward, faster, into the suffocating dark, praying with everything left in me that love could outrun death tonight.

THE JEFFERSON HOUSE

The night erupted into chaos as Henry Jefferson squeezed the trigger, the shotgun roaring like thunder trapped inside the house. The muzzle flash lit the living room in a brief, blinding strobe, and buckshot tore through the shattered front window, shredding leaves from the shrubs and sending the nearest hooded figures scrambling for cover. They dove behind fence posts and low hedges, their white robes flapping like startled wings. Glass rained onto the porch in a glittering cascade, tinkling sharply against the wooden planks. One dropped torch hissed and sputtered as it landed in the damp grass, its flame dying with a weak plume of smoke that curled upward into the frigid air.

From the back of the house came the sudden, frantic pounding of fists on the door. Three Klansmen rammed their shoulders against it, the wood groaning under the assault. Ruth, heart slamming against her ribs, seized the nearest kitchen chair and swung it with all her strength. The legs cracked across the first intruder's hooded skull as he forced the door open a few inches, the impact sending a jolt up her arms. He staggered, cursing, and she kicked the door shut with a desperate shove, slamming the deadbolt home just as the butt of a rifle smashed against the knob from the other side. Splinters flew. She threw her full weight against the door again, shoulder burning with the effort, and felt the man on the other side stumble backward into his companions.

"Henry!" Her voice cracked over the deafening gunfire, raw with terror.

"I got the front!" he bellowed back, voice steady despite the strain. "Hold that door, Ruth! Whatever it takes!"

A side window exploded inward with a violent crash, shards spraying across the floor like deadly hail. Two Klansmen clambered through the jagged frame, boots crunching on broken glass, faces hidden beneath those hateful hoods. Henry whirled, pumping the shotgun in one fluid motion, and fired point-blank. The blast filled the room with acrid smoke and the deafening boom that made Ruth's ears ring. Both men were hurled backward through the window, bodies twisting mid-air before they slammed onto the lawn with sickening thuds, groans rising faintly over the chaos.

Henry was not merely defending his home. He was a wall of defiance, every shot a refusal to let their poison cross his threshold, to let it touch his family. Upstairs, in the dim closet of the main bedroom, Lily pressed her back against the wall, arms locked around her trembling little brother. His small body shook with silent sobs, face buried in her nightgown, the fabric damp with his tears. The air smelled of gunpowder drifting up through the floorboards, sharp and choking.

"It's okay," Lily whispered, her own voice quivering as another gunshot shook the house. "We're safe here. Just stay quiet, baby. Stay with me."

Outside, the night grew eerily still for a heartbeat. Then came the low murmurs, the rustle of fabric, the scrape of boots on earth. The white shapes shifted and regrouped in the flickering torchlight, swirling like malevolent ghosts gathering courage for the next assault. Tension coiled tighter; the air was thick with the stench of smoke, sweat, and impending violence.

Inside, Henry's hands trembled as he fumbled fresh shells into the shotgun, the brass casings slick with sweat. Ruth braced her bleeding shoulder against the back door, every muscle screaming, breath coming in shallow gasps. Upstairs, Lily's blood ran cold as she heard faint footsteps crunching directly beneath the bedroom window, slow and deliberate.

They were surrounded. Outnumbered. The seconds stretched like hours, each one heavier than the last.

Henry racked another round with a sharp metallic clack and fired through the ruined front window. Two Klansmen flung themselves behind the fence, but the third was too slow. The buckshot caught him in the leg; his agonized scream pierced the night as he collapsed, clutching the wound, dragging himself pitifully toward cover behind a stump, leaving a dark trail on the grass.

Henry ducked as a bullet whined past his ear, embedding in the wall with a puff of plaster. His chest heaved, lungs burning, strength ebbing with every passing moment. Ten to one. Maybe more. He could feel the odds closing in like a noose.

"Henry!" Ruth's frantic cry cut through from the kitchen. "They're coming around back again!"

"I see them!" he shouted, pivoting toward the sound. But in that split second of divided attention, the front door burst open with a splintering crack. Two Klansmen rushed up the porch steps. The first drove the butt of his rifle into Henry's ribs with brutal force, the impact folding him forward with a grunt of pain that stole his breath. The second tackled him full-force, slamming him to the floorboards. The shotgun spun from his grasp, clattering uselessly across the room.

Ruth's scream echoed his name, high and desperate. More hooded figures poured through the breached entryway, boots thundering. One dropped a heavy knee into Henry's chest, pinning him down, the weight crushing the air from his lungs. Another raised a clenched fist, ready to bring it crashing down.

Then, from the darkness, headlights blazed to life like twin suns, cutting through the night and flooding the yard in harsh white glare.

Jesse Boone's truck roared forward, engine snarling, tires spitting gravel as it barreled straight toward the house. It smashed through the side wall with catastrophic force, wood beams splintering like matchsticks, plaster exploding in clouds of dust, furniture shattering under the onslaught of shrieking metal and flying debris. The entire house shuddered violently, floorboards bucking beneath them. Upstairs, Lily screamed as the ceiling groaned and dust rained down.

Henry coughed through the choking haze, struggling to rise, but the Klansmen ground him harder into the floor, their grips like iron. Jesse stumbled from the crumpled cab, blood trickling from a gash on his forehead, rifle clutched unsteadily in dazed hands.

For one agonizing moment, everything hung suspended in choking dust and flickering torchlight. Hope flickered, fragile and dying.

Then another window shattered somewhere above, glass cascading like a deadly rain, and a new roar of gunfire split the night.

CALEB POV

I didn't feel the glass slicing into my arms or the sting of fresh cuts as I launched myself through the jagged remains of the front window. Shards exploded around me like deadly confetti, crunching under my knees as I hit the floor hard and rolled through a choking cloud of plaster dust and gunpowder haze. The air reeked of scorched wood and blood, thick enough to taste on my tongue. My ears rang from the endless gunfire, but I was up in an instant, heart slamming against my ribs.

Two hooded shapes lunged out of the swirling dust, white robes streaked with dirt and shadow. The first one seized my shirt in a brutal grip, yanking me forward with a snarl I could smell through his hood, sour sweat and whiskey. I drove my forehead into the soft cartilage of his nose. The wet crunch vibrated through my skull, followed by his high, muffled scream as hot blood sprayed across my face. He dropped like a sack, clutching his ruined face.

The second swung a crowbar in a vicious arc. I ducked on instinct, feeling the cold iron whistle past my ear close enough to stir my hair. The momentum carried him forward, and I buried my fist deep into his gut. Air whooshed from his lungs in a strangled gasp. Before he could double over, I hooked a hard right across his jaw. Bone met bone with a sharp crack, and he crumpled to the floorboards, hood twisting as he fell.

A third came roaring out of the smoke, knife gleaming in the flickering torchlight from outside, blade raised high for a killing plunge. Time slowed. My hand moved without thought, snatching the pistol tucked in my waistband. The grip was warm, slick with my own sweat. I brought it up, thumb flicking the safety, and squeezed the trigger once. The gunshot was deafening in the confined space, muzzle flash blinding white. The Klansman jerked backward, knife spinning away as he collapsed in a heap, dark stain blooming across his chest.

My hands shook violently now, the pistol trembling in my grip. The smell of fresh powder burned my nostrils, and bile rose in my throat. I hated this. I hated every second of it. But they had come for Lily, for her family, and I would burn the world down before I let them touch her.

I spun toward the porch where Mr. Jefferson was struggling to rise, blood trickling from a cut on his temple. I grabbed his arm, hauling him up. "Come on, sir, stay with me!"

He gripped my forearm hard, eyes fierce through the pain. We stood back to back in the ruined living room, me with the stolen pistol raised, him empty-handed but unbowed, his breathing ragged but steady. Outside, more hooded figures regrouped in the yard, torches casting long, dancing shadows. Mr. Jefferson glanced over his shoulder at me, voice rough. "Glad you made it, son."

"Wasn't gonna let you fight alone," I said, voice raw, tasting copper and dust.

We braced for the next wave.

Jesse Boone staggered up from the wreckage of his truck, face twisted in rage and something that looked sickeningly like betrayal. Dust coated his hair and clothes, blood streaking from a gash above his eye. He raised his rifle with shaking hands, the barrel wavering as he leveled it at me through the haze of settling debris.

"Caleb!" His voice cracked over the groans of wounded men and the crackle of scattered flames. "Stand down! Don't make me, don't make me do this!"

I didn't raise the pistol toward him. Couldn't. Not Jesse. Instead, I turned my wrist in one desperate motion, aiming past him into the kitchen where the old gas stove hissed ominously, its pilot light still flickering blue. I pulled the trigger.

The explosion was instantaneous and cataclysmic. A deafening roar swallowed everything as a massive fireball erupted outward, orange and white and hungry. The shockwave slammed into us like a freight train, hurling Jesse backward off his feet. He flew through the air, rifle spinning away, before crashing hard into the shattered remains of the living room wall.

Ruth, braced in the kitchen doorway, saw the muzzle flash a split second before the world ignited. She threw herself flat behind the heavy oak table, arms covering her head as the blast ripped through the room. Heat scorched the air above her, searing hot, carrying the stench of burning gas and splintered wood. Debris pelted her back like hail, shards of metal and flaming fragments raining down. The floor buckled beneath her, and for a terrifying moment, she thought the entire house would collapse.

Upstairs, the explosion hit like God's own hammer. Lily and little Isaiah were huddled together in the dark closet, her arms locked tight around him. The floor lurched violently, throwing them against the wall. Dust poured from the ceiling in choking clouds, and the deafening boom rattled their teeth. Isaias wailed in terror, a high, piercing sound that cut straight to Lily's heart. She pulled him closer, pressing his face into her shoulder to muffle his cries and shield him from the plaster raining down.

"It's okay, it's okay," she gasped, voice trembling as much as her body, coughing through the thick dust that coated her throat. Her ears rang, the world muffled and distant, but she held him tighter, rocking him as the house groaned and settled around them.

Outside, Klansmen near the porch were flung backward like rag dolls, some sheets bursting into flame as they rolled screaming across the grass. The shockwave shattered what few windows remained intact, glass spraying outward in glittering arcs. Henry threw himself over me, his body a shield as chunks of burning debris clattered around us, the heat blistering against my skin.

In the sudden, ringing silence that followed, flames crackled hungrily, and the night smelled only of destruction.

Outside, the remaining Klansmen reeled in the choking smoke and flickering flames, coughing and blinking against the stinging grit that hung thick in the air. Their white robes were torn and soot-streaked, torches sputtering weakly on the trampled grass. Groans rose from the wounded, sharp with pain and confusion, as they struggled to regroup in the acrid haze.

But one man stood unmoved amid the chaos.

From behind the crumpled truck, Ezekiel Whitlock rose with deliberate slowness, his eyes blazing like hot coals in the firelight. The metallic tang of blood and burning wood filled his nostrils, fueling the rage twisting his features. He reached into the truck bed, fingers closing around the cold, polished stock of a long black shotgun. His jaw locked tight, nostrils flaring with each furious breath. Everything was unraveling. His perfect plan was shattered. His authority is crumbling. Worst of all, his own son had betrayed him in front of everyone, publicly, unforgivably. Hate poured off him in palpable waves, thick and venomous. He racked the shotgun with a sharp, ominous clack that cut through the night and marched toward the ruined doorway, boots crunching over broken glass and splintered wood.

The house shuddered violently again as another shotgun blast ripped through the siding, filling the air with the sharp bite of gunpowder and fresh splinters. Mr. Jefferson and I fought desperately against the last two Klansmen, forcing their way through the front. I drove my boot into one man's knee with a sickening crack, feeling the joint give as he howled and collapsed. Mr. Jefferson swung a jagged chair leg like a club, smashing it across the other's mouth. Teeth scattered across the floorboards with a wet clatter, blood spraying in a warm arc.

For one fleeting heartbeat, amid the sweat and dust and labored breaths, it felt like we had won.

Then came the single, earth-shaking gunshot, louder than all the rest, echoing like doom inside the walls.

A scream tore through the air. I whipped around just in time to see Mrs. Jefferson, Ruth, jerk backward as if struck by an invisible hammer. A gaping hole bloomed red in her chest, dark blood soaking her dress in an instant. She crumpled near the kitchen doorway, her body hitting the floor with a soft, final thud that echoed in my soul.

"Ruth!" Mr. Jefferson's voice shattered, raw and anguished, a sound no man should ever have to make. He let the chair leg fall from his numb fingers, clattering uselessly, and sprinted to her side. I stood frozen, the world narrowing to a cold, hollow point. Blood pooled beneath her, warm and glistening on the tiles, its coppery scent flooding the room.

He scooped her into his arms, cradling her against his chest as he rocked on his knees, murmuring her name over and over like a prayer that could pull her back. "Ruth... Ruth, no... stay with me, love..." His voice broke into sobs, profound and wrenching, tears cutting clean tracks through the grime on his face. I had seen hate destroy before, but never like this. Never a good woman, a mother, bleeding out on her own floor while her husband begged the heavens for mercy that would not come.

Something inside Henry Jefferson fractured then, visible in the way his shoulders sagged, in the hollow grief filling his eyes. He looked up at me, face etched with a sorrow too vast for words, too unfair for this world.

"Caleb..." His voice trembled, barely above a whisper. "Son... listen to me."

"No," I choked out, shaking my head violently, tears burning my own eyes. "No, don't say it. We need you. Lily needs you. Please."

He reached out with blood-slick hands and grabbed my shirtfront, pulling me down to him. His grip was fierce despite the weakness creeping in. "If you're half the man I think you are... protect my babies." His breath hitched, ragged and wet. "Protect Lily. And Isaiah. Promise me, Caleb. Promise."

"Mr. Jefferson..."

"Promise me."

I squeezed my eyes shut, the weight of it crushing me. I didn't want this burden. Didn't want to leave him here to die. But Lily. Isaiah. Their faces flashed in my mind, innocent and terrified. My throat closed with grief. "I promise," I whispered, voice cracking like thin ice.

He nodded once, a faint spark of pride cutting through the pain, then shoved me toward the stairs with the last of his strength. "Go. Now."

I ran.

Behind me, I heard the metallic scrape as he reloaded his shotgun one final time, the shells clicking home with trembling fingers. Then the booming roar as he opened fire again, each blast a defiant scream, holding the doorway like a lion guarding his pride with nothing left to lose.

I charged up the creaking steps two at a time, heart pounding in my ears, and burst into the bedroom. Lily crouched in the corner, arms wrapped protectively around little Isaiah, his small face buried in her shoulder, muffling his whimpers. The room smelled of dust and fear-sweat. Her eyes, wide and red-rimmed, lit with desperate relief when she saw me.

"Caleb!" she breathed, voice barely audible. "Is Mama...? Is it over?"

I couldn't speak the words. The truth must have shown on my face, streaked with tears and blood. Her breath caught sharply, a soft, wounded sound, and she pulled Isaias tighter, fresh tears spilling down her cheeks.

"We have to go," I urged, voice low and urgent, thick with the grief I swallowed down. "Your daddy... he told me to get you out. He's buying us time."

"What about Dad?" she demanded, voice rising in panic, but already breaking.

I shook my head, the pain too raw. Her face crumpled completely, a silent sob shaking her body, but she nodded, gathering Isaiah closer. He clung to her, confused and terrified, small hands fisting in her nightgown.

I led them quietly into the back hallway, moving fast but carefully, avoiding every loose board that might creak and betray us. The air grew heavier with smoke drifting up from below. Downstairs, Henry's shotgun thundered until the final click of an empty chamber echoed like a death knell.

Then came the low, heavy thud of the front door splintering fully open, boots on wood. A body hitting the floor hard.

I risked a glance through the railing, my blood turning to ice.

My father, Ezekiel, stepped through the wreckage like a predator finally cornering its prey, shotgun barrel still trailing smoke. He tossed it aside with a clatter and cracked his knuckles, the sound sharp in the sudden quiet.

Henry staggered to his feet across the room, chest heaving, blood staining his shirt from earlier wounds. But he stood tall, unyielding. "You took my wife," he growled, voice hoarse with fury and loss.

"And you took my boy," Ezekiel spat, venom dripping from every word. "You poisoned him against his own blood. Turned him rotten."

Henry let out a bitter, broken laugh that held no humor. "Your boy walked in here a better man than you'll ever be."

My father's face contorted, pure hate twisting his features into something monstrous. Without warning, he lunged.

They crashed together in the shattered living room, fists flying, bodies slamming into broken furniture and fallen beams with grunts and thuds that shook the floor beneath us. Henry fought like a man possessed, grief fueling every blow. He landed heavy punches, driving my father back, knocking him to the floor. Again. And again. Blood sprayed from split lips, knuckles raw and bleeding.

We reached the back door. I eased it open a crack, cool night air rushing in, carrying the distant wail of sirens. But from the corner of my eye, I saw it. My father's hand slips into his boot.

"No..." The whisper escaped me, horror clawing my throat.

Steel flashed. The knife plunged deep into Henry's ribs with a sickening sound. Henry gasped, a wet, choking breath. His eyes widened in shock and pain as he staggered, hands clutching the hilt. He dropped to his knees, then forward onto the floorboards, blood spreading beneath him in a dark, glistening pool that reflected the flickering flames.

Lily's sharp gasp behind me turned into a muffled cry. She lunged toward the stairs, but I caught her, clamping my hand gently but firmly over her mouth, pulling her and Isaiah against me. Her body shook with silent, wrenching sobs. Isaiah whimpered, sensing the horror.

My promise.

My promise to a dying man.

Tears blurred my vision, chest burning with a grief that threatened to swallow me whole. But I dragged them through the back door into the cold night, the grass wet and sharp underfoot. Behind us, my father stood over Henry's body, breathing hard, a dark satisfaction on his face.

I didn't look back. Couldn't. The sounds of that final collapse echoed in my ears, in my heart. Henry Jefferson was gone, a good man murdered for daring to love. The weight of his trust, his last words, pressed on me like the night itself. Breaking that promise would mean losing everything he died for. So I kept moving, holding Lily and Isaiah close, into the darkness, carrying their father's final gift: a chance to live.

CHAPTER TWELVE

We ran.

I didn't stop until the trees closed thick around us, branches whipping my face, roots snagging at my boots. My lungs were raw fire, my legs trembling like they might give out any second. Lily kept pace, one hand clamped tight around Isaiah's small fingers. The boy stumbled but didn't cry, just clung to her and ran.

Finally, we burst into the small clearing where the old clubhouse stood, the one Jesse and I had hammered together as kids out of scrap wood and big dreams. Vines had claimed most of it now; the boards were warped and gray, and the roof sagged. It wasn't much. But it was hidden.

I kicked the swollen door open with my shoulder.

"Inside," I panted.

Lily guided Isaiah first, pulling him close. I followed and shoved the door shut, sliding the rusty bolt with a scrape that sounded too loud in the quiet.

The second it locked, the last of my strength left me.

I staggered into the tiny bathroom corner, braced my hands on the cracked sink, and stared at my reflection in the broken mirror. Blood streaked my face. My eyes looked hollow.

Then it hit me all at once.

I broke.

Not quite tears. Not the kind you hide. I sobbed like something inside had torn loose, shoulders shaking, breath hitching. For Henry. For Ruth. For the blood on my hands and the family I couldn't save, for dragging Lily and Isaiah into this hell.

I didn't hear her come in.

Soft footsteps. Then Lily's hands cupped my face, gentle but firm. She pulled me to her and kissed me, hard and desperate, like she was pouring life back into me. When she drew back, her forehead rested against mine, both of us breathing the same air.

"You didn't fail," she whispered, voice fierce through her own tears. "You saved us. You hear me? You saved us."

Her fingers moved to my back, tracing the raised welts and cuts with trembling care. She found an old rag, wet it from a leaky faucet, and cleaned the wounds slowly, wincing every time I flinched. Neither of us spoke. We didn't need to.

Isaiah appeared in the doorway, small and shaking. "Is it over?" he asked, voice barely there.

I knelt, ignoring the burn in my back, and opened my arms. He ran into them. I held him tight, feeling his little body shake against mine.

"You're safe now," I told him, meaning every word. "I've got you. Nothing's gonna happen to you. I promise."

He buried his face in my shoulder and finally let the tears come.

When he drifted off, exhausted, Lily laid him on an old blanket in the corner and sat watch. I dug through the dusty trunk we'd used as kids for treasure. Inside were things we'd thought made us men back then: a couple of old .22 rifles, a revolver we'd sworn was just for show, boxes of ammo gone green at the edges, a hunting knife, and a coffee tin stuffed with crumpled bills we'd saved from odd jobs.

Enough to get us far.

I loaded the duffel, checked the revolver Mama had given me, and helped Lily wake Isaiah. We slipped out the back, creeping through the brush until we hit the creek. Cold water soaked our shoes, but it covered our tracks.

On the far side, half a mile down the dirt road, sat one of the Klan's abandoned trucks, left behind when the boys had piled into others. Keys still in it.

I turned the key quickly, the engine coughing to life. Lily buckled Isaiah in the back, then slid in beside me.

I pulled onto the road and pointed the truck north, away from town, away from everything I'd ever known.

For the first time, the wheel was in my hands. The road ahead was dark and uncertain, but it was mine to choose.

They would come looking. I knew that.

But tonight, we were free.

Jesse POV

Hours later, Jesse Boone led the convoy back to the old clubhouse, tires crunching slowly over the dirt path. The place looked abandoned in the moonlight, vines choking the walls, no light, no sound. Too still.

Jesse's heart hammered as he jumped out first, rifle in hand. He kicked the door wide and stormed inside, half-hoping, half-dreading what he'd find.

Empty.

The trunk yawned open, lid thrown back. Gun racks stripped bare. The tin box was pried apart, and the cash was gone. Fresh boot prints led out the back, already fading into the brush.

Tommy stepped in behind him, whistling low. "Looks like somebody cleaned us out."

Jesse didn't answer. He knew. The truth settled cold and heavy in his gut before anyone spoke it.

"It was Caleb," he said, voice barely above a whisper.

Ezekiel shoved past the others, eyes wild with fury. "What did you say?"

Jesse met his gaze, throat tight. "He took the guns. The money. One of the trucks."

Ezekiel stared at the empty racks for a long moment, face twisting from shock to something darker. When he spoke, his voice came low and venomous.

"My own son... is a traitor."

The words hung in the dusty air like a death sentence. The other men shifted uneasily, their eyes on the floor.

Jesse felt it twist inside him: guilt like acid, regret sharp as broken glass. Caleb had been his brother. And Jesse had helped put the whip in their hands.

But the feeling hardened fast into something colder. Resolve.

Ezekiel crossed to the old wall phone and dialed a number few men knew. His knuckles went white on the receiver.

"National Operations," a clipped voice answered.

"This is Grand Dragon Whitlock, East Texas Chapter," Ezekiel growled. "We got a rogue. My son. Caleb Whitlock. He aided a Negro family. Stole weapons and cash. He's armed and on the run. I want him handled."

A pause. Papers rustling on the other end.

"Identity confirmed. Description and photo on file. Bounty authorized."

Ezekiel hung up without another word.

Washington, D.C. — Klan National Headquarters

Deep underground, in a cold war room lit by harsh bulbs, maps covered the walls alongside crosses and rifles. A massive corkboard dominated one corner, strung with red yarn and photographs of targets.

The secretary pulled Caleb's old file photo, a grainy shot of a fourteen-year-old boy grinning beside Jesse after a shooting match, and pinned it to the board's bottom row.

She stamped it in bold red:

BOUNTY: $25,000

TARGET: CALEB WHITLOCK

STATUS: ACTIVE

A typed memo followed, sent to every chapter across the country:

SUBJECT: TRAITOR REQUIRING TERMINATION

ALL KLANNERS AND AFFILIATED ASSETS ARE AUTHORIZED TO ENGAGE

She pressed a buzzer.

Three doors down, a handful of hard-eyed men looked up from cleaning weapons. Their handler entered and slapped the fresh photo onto the table.

"New priority target," he said. "Whitlock's own boy turned. Bring him in any way you can. Dead preferred."

Back in Texas — The Hideout

Ezekiel turned from the phone, face carved from stone.

Jesse stepped forward, voice steady despite the storm inside. "Sir... let me lead the hunt."

Ezekiel studied him long and cold. "You failed once already."

Jesse didn't flinch. "I won't fail again—Caleb's my responsibility. I know how he thinks. Where he'll go."

Ezekiel tapped his fingers on the table, eyes narrowed. Then he nodded once, sharply.

"Fine. But hear me clear, boy. You bring him back, or you don't come back at all."

Jesse met his gaze, jaw set. "I won't fail."

The men loaded rifles and torches. Engines roared to life.

The hunt was on.

CHAPTER THIRTEEN

Mary Beth Hollander studied her reflection in the girls' restroom mirror, adjusting the satin ribbon in her golden curls for what felt like the tenth time. Everything was in place. Pale pink lipstick gleamed on her lips. Her dress fit her body perfectly. Her smile was the one every Southern girl learned early. Sweet. Inviting. Unbreakable. Perfect. Pretty. Desired. For a Hollander, perfection was not vanity. It was an obligation.

She had grown up on the stories, spoken softly at family dinners like scripture. Her great-grandfather, Richard Hollander, known as Judge, had come home from the Civil War with a stiff jaw and hardened eyes. He was not a real judge, but the name stuck because he decided things, and others obeyed. After Reconstruction, he took control of the town piece by piece, claiming prime farmland on the outskirts. The Black family who owned it disappeared one night, and no one ever spoke of them again. That land became the foundation of the Hollander fortune.

Her grandfather, Earl, expanded it into influence, donating to churches and festivals while quietly deciding who received loans and who did not. Respect flowed in one direction. Obedience to the other. Her father, Charles, carried the legacy into City Hall, speaking openly about order and purity while shaping policy behind closed doors. Her mother ruled the social calendar with iron grace, teaching Mary Beth that beauty was leverage, marriage was strategy, and the family name was a crown that must never be tarnished.

Mary Beth wanted more than approval. She wanted power.

In this town, no one held more of it than the Whitlocks. Especially Caleb. He was the heir, the future, the face behind the hood. Love did not matter. Fear did. Influence did. As his wife, she would be untouchable. She would rule quietly while he ruled openly. The Hollander name would endure.

She smoothed her skirt once more and left the restroom, confidence steady in her chest.

The cafeteria roared with noise. She spotted Caleb at the boys' table, cards fanned in his hand, laughter spilling around him. She approached with practiced ease and leaned against the edge of the table, as it belonged to her.

"Caleb Whitlock," she said, voice soft and sweet. "You want to walk me home after school?"

He barely looked up. "Uh, no. Thanks, though."

The words struck hard. Her smile faltered for half a breath.

"Oh," she said lightly. "Are you busy?"

"Something like that."

Heat rushed to her face. She smiled anyway, brighter than before, then turned and walked away, posture perfect. When she reached her friends, their laughter followed her.

"He shut you down," one said, hand over her mouth.

"Imagine," another snickered. "The great Mary Beth Hollander, rejected like yesterday's news."

Mary Beth laughed with them, a light tinkling sound, while her nails bit into her palms beneath the table.

A few days later, she went to Harrison's Diner, sure she would see him. Caleb was always there. She slid into the booth beside Jesse and the boys, her curls shining, a smile on her face that seemed effortless.

"Y'all seen Caleb?" she asked.

Jesse shook his head. "Not today."

Then Tommy stiffened. "Jess. Look."

Mary Beth followed their gaze out the window. Caleb walked alone beneath the streetlights, coming from the wrong direction, the colored side of town.

Something cold curled in her stomach.

Two days later, the town was aware of everything. Secrets did not survive here. By noon, the whispers had turned into open talk.

"Did you hear?" a girl said in the hallway. "Caleb dumped Mary Beth for Lily Jefferson."

The laughter stung like smoke. She kept walking. At lunch, it was worse.

"Imagine being replaced like that."

"Guess she wasn't special after all."

Even grown folks joined in, murmuring on church steps and in grocery aisles.

"What a fall for the Hollanders."

At home, the house felt brittle. Her mother cried in the parlor, clutching a handkerchief. Her father paced the study, furious and humiliated.

"Hollanders don't get humiliated like this. We're better than that. We built this town!"

Mary Beth went to her room and locked the door. She stared at her reflection. The curls. The lipstick. The smile that had always worked.

Not anymore.

This was not about a boy. It was about legacy. Caleb had chosen Lily Jefferson and, in doing so, had dragged the Hollander name through the dirt. She had not just been rejected. She had been replaced.

Rage settled into something colder. Sharper.

She would not cry. She would not beg. She would not fade quietly into someone else's story.

She would restore what was hers, and when she was finished, no one would ever laugh at the name Hollander again.

JESSE POV

Jesse Boone's room was a wreck, like a twister had ripped through it and left nothing standing. Drawers hung open, clothes spilled across the floor in tangled heaps, boots half laced and kicked aside. The mattress sat crooked, yanked off center from where he'd dragged his rifle case out from underneath.

He crammed shirts and spare magazines into his duffel with rough, trembling hands. He told himself the shakes were from adrenaline, not nerves. Not fear. This was justice, plain and simple. Righteous work. But his fingers brushed something buried under a pile of faded school papers. A small, worn photograph.

He stopped cold.

The edges were frayed and yellowed, colors bled out from too many summers in the sun. Two little boys grinned back at him, barefoot and filthy, arms slung around each other's shoulders like they owned the world. Mud caked their faces and clothes, but their eyes shone bright with unbreakable trust.

Jesse's throat closed up. The memory came without warning.

The Sabine River had been swollen from days of rain, brown water rushing hard and fast. Jesse had been ten and full of fire, daring the current like it was a challenge meant just for him. He remembered how cold the water felt around his ankles, then his knees, then his waist. He remembered laughing when the pull tugged at him, how it made him feel big and strong.

Caleb had been on the bank, barefoot, too, yelling. "Jesse, get back here. That water ain't playing' around."

Jesse had waved him off and stepped deeper.

The river dropped away beneath his feet without warning. One second, there was ground, the next, there was nothing. The current seized him and yanked him under so hard it knocked the air clean out of his chest. The water filled his ears. The world went dark and roaring all at once.

He remembered the panic more than anything. The way his arms flailed uselessly. The way the light above fractured and warped the harder he fought. His lungs burned and screamed. In that moment, he knew with a sick certainty that he was about to die.

Then a hand locked around his wrist.

Strong. Desperate. Real.

Caleb.

Jesse felt himself being dragged upward, inch by inch. He remembered the strain on Caleb's face when he broke the surface, his teeth clenched, his skinny arms shaking as he hauled Jesse back to the bank. They collapsed together in the mud, coughing and choking, river water pouring from Jesse's mouth.

Caleb had hovered over him, soaked and shaking, fear written all over his face. "If you ever scare me like that again," he had said, voice cracking, "and I'll beat your ass myself. What would I do without you?"

Jesse had laughed, even as tears streamed down his face, because Caleb had always been there. Always. They were brothers. Nothing could touch them.

Back in the room, Jesse stared at the photograph until his vision began to blur. His grip tightened around it.

"Why'd you do it?" he whispered. "Why her?"

The words fell apart in his throat. Tears slid down his face, hot and humiliating. He hated them. Hated the weakness. The ache cut deeper than anything he had ever known.

Something inside him snapped.

He crushed the photograph in his fist, paper crumpling as he dragged his sleeve across his face. Enough. Whatever Caleb had been to him, whatever they had shared, it was gone.

Jesse zipped the duffel shut with a violent jerk that stung his fingers. This was not about duty anymore. It was not about loyalty or blood. Caleb had taken the only real family Jesse had ever known and discarded it.

For that, there would be a price.

He carried the bag downstairs, each step heavy and final. His mother stood at the bottom, her hands twisting in her apron, eyes red and swollen.

She rushed forward and wrapped him in a fierce embrace. "Be careful," she whispered. "Please. Come back to me."

He stiffened, then let her hold him a moment longer. Her familiar scent wrapped around him, the last thread of home pulling tight.

His father stood behind her, arms crossed, chest puffed out. "That's my boy," he said proudly. "Doing what needs doing. Showing this town the Boone name still means something."

Jesse nodded once and stepped outside.

The screen door slammed behind him, sharp and final. The night air hit cold against his face.

That was when he saw Mary Beth Hollander.

She stood beside his truck, a small suitcase clutched in both hands. Her curls were pinned tight. Her lipstick was a deep, violent red. Her eyes held something hard and shining.

"Mary Beth," he said. "What are you doing here?"

"I'm coming with you."

"No." The word came out fast. "This ain't your fight."

Her smile was thin and brittle. "He humiliated me. The whole town knows. They're laughing. Whispering that even a colored girl was worth more than me."

Her voice trembled, not with weakness, but fury. "My family built this town. And now our name's a joke because Caleb Whitlock chose her."

She stepped closer. "They took everything I was raised to be. I need to see them pay."

He exhaled slowly and unlocked the passenger door.

"Get in."

She climbed inside without a word, spine straight, suitcase in her lap like armor.

Jesse pulled the crumpled photograph from his pocket one last time. Two muddy boys grinning like nothing could ever break them.

He shoved it away, slammed the door, and started the engine.

The truck surged forward into the dark.

There was no turning back now.

CALEB POV

I'd been driving so long the highway lines blurred into one endless gray ribbon, headlights cutting through the dark like a knife that never found anything to cut. My eyes stung with every blink, gritty and raw, and the signs we passed had stopped meaning anything hours ago. Texas, Oklahoma, maybe Arkansas by now. I didn't know. I didn't care. Just north. Just away. Away from the blood, the smoke, the faces of men I'd once called brothers.

Lily sat beside me, Isaiah curled asleep in her lap, his small chest rising and falling under her steady hand. His soft breaths were the only gentle sound in the cab, cutting through the low rumble of the engine and the whistle of wind through the cracked window. The night before clung to me like damp clothes: the crack of gunfire, Ruth's body crumpling, Henry's last promise burning in my ears. I hadn't slept. Not once. Every time I closed my eyes, I saw them coming.

"Caleb," Lily said quietly, her voice pulling me back. "Pull over."

"I'm fine," I rasped, gripping the wheel tighter. My knuckles ached.

"No, you're not." She reached over, fingers brushing my arm. "You're shaking. Pull over before you run us off the road."

She was right. My hands trembled on the wheel, vision swimming at the edges. I eased off the highway at the next exit, tires humming over gravel until a faded neon sign flickered ahead: VACANCY. The motel was old, paint peeling in long curls, doors the color of rust. A single bulb buzzed over the office like a tired firefly.

We checked in with cash, no questions asked. The clerk barely looked up. I carried Isaiah inside while Lily held the door. The room smelled of stale smoke, cheap pine cleaner, and the faint metallic tang of the ancient air conditioner rattling in the wall. Two sagging beds, a lamp with a crooked shade, curtains thin enough to let the neon bleed through in pulses of red.

Lily lay Isaiah on the far bed, tucking the thin blanket around him. She kissed his forehead, lingering a moment, then turned to me.

I sank onto the edge of the other bed, elbows on my knees, head dropping into my hands. My whole body buzzed, a live wire of fear and exhaustion and guilt I couldn't shut off. Every muscle screamed. My back throbbed where the whip had torn skin. I felt filthy with it all, unworthy of the quiet in this room, unworthy of them.

Lily knelt in front of me, hands gentle on my knees. "Caleb. Look at me."

I lifted my head. Her eyes were red-rimmed but steady, full of something that made the storm inside me pause.

"You don't have to hold everything together right now," she whispered.

"I'm trying," I said, voice cracking like dry earth. "God, Lily, I'm trying so hard. Your parents... I couldn't... I promised him and I still—"

"Shh." She cupped my face, thumbs brushing the stubble on my cheeks. "You got us out. You kept your promise. That's enough for tonight."

Her touch unraveled me. The walls I'd built mile after mile came crumbling down. I leaned forward until my forehead rested against hers, breathing her vanilla and warm skin and the faint sweetness of the lotion she used on Isaiah. For the first time since the world caught fire, I felt something close to safe.

She climbed onto the bed beside me and pulled me down with her. I let her guide my head to her shoulder, her arms wrapping around me like she could shield me from everything chasing us. I curled into her, fingers clutching the fabric of her dress, afraid that if I let go, I'd wake up and find it all a dream.

"It's okay," she murmured into my hair. "We're safe right now. Just breathe."

I did. Slow, shaky breaths that finally evened out. The hum of the air conditioner, the distant drone of trucks on the highway, and Isaiah's soft snoring across the room. It all blurred together.

My last clear thought was how right she felt against me, how her heartbeat under my ear was the steadiest thing I'd ever known.

Then sleep took me, deep and dreamless, the first real peace I'd felt in what seemed like forever.

Sometime later, she shifted gently, easing us both down until we lay side by side. Her head settled against mine, one arm draped over me, breath warm on my cheek. In that dim, flickering motel room miles from everything we'd lost, we slept tangled together, two kids carrying the weight of the world and refusing to let it crush us. Not yet.

CHAPTER FOURTEEN

I woke before the sun; the room was still shrouded in shadow. The air smelled of old sheets and the faint metallic hum of the air conditioner rattling in the wall. Lily lay curled against me, warm and solid, one hand spread over my chest like she had held me there all night. Isaiah slept beside her, small and peaceful, his breath slow and even.

For a moment, I let myself believe we were safe.

I eased out from under her arm, careful not to wake either of them. My back screamed as I moved, the welts pulling tight, but I swallowed the pain.

"I'll check us out," I whispered.

Lily stirred, eyes barely open. "I'll get him ready."

Outside, the courtyard lay empty beneath the gray light before dawn. Gravel crunched softly under my boots. No birds yet. No traffic on the highway. The silence pressed close, wrong in a way I could not explain.

Halfway to the office, I passed an open room. A housekeeper stood inside, wiping the bathroom mirror. Something about him stopped me cold. His shoulders were too broad for the faded uniform; the fabric stretched tight across his back. His belt sat high and stiff, as if it were hiding weight it should not. His shoes were black tactical boots, scuffed but heavy. Not the kind worn by men who cleaned rooms.

I kept walking, forcing my pace to stay steady, every nerve screaming.

The office bell rang when I stepped inside, too loud in the quiet. A man stood behind the counter, mid-thirties, clean-shaven, with a smile that never reached his eyes. His motel shirt was buttoned incorrectly, and his nametag was crooked. The counter was bare. No register. No coffee pot. No clutter.

"Morning," he said, smooth as glass.

"Morning." I kept my voice light. "Checking out of room twelve."

He hesitated. Just long enough. "Name?"

My pulse jumped. A ten-room motel, and he did not know his guests.

"Whitlock. Caleb Whitlock."

He blinked slowly. "Cash, right?"

Everyone paid cash. I pushed once more. "What time do you start the coffee?"

He froze.

The smile vanished, and his hand came up fast from under the counter. A knife flashed in the dim light, curved and military sharp. He slashed. I jumped back, blocking with my forearm, pain tearing up my arm. I grabbed his wrist and drove it down hard. The blade skittered across the floor.

He lunged at me. We crashed into a rack of maps and brochures, paper exploding around us. I slammed an elbow into his ribs, rolled with him, pinned his weight, and drove my fist into his face. Twice. He headbutted me, and white stars burst across my vision.

We grappled on the floor, breath ragged, sweat and blood slick between us. I twisted his arm until something popped, and slammed him down. He went limp.

Gunfire erupted outside.

Glass shattered. Bullets chewed through the lobby walls, splintering wood and punching holes through the counter. I dove behind it as dust and plaster filled the air. My ears rang until the world went hollow.

When I looked up, my stomach dropped.

Behind the desk lay the real clerk. A middle-aged woman slumped sideways, a single bullet hole centered in her forehead. Blood had dried dark along her temple. She had been dead for hours.

I reached out with a shaking hand and closed her eyes. "I'm sorry."

Footsteps crunched through broken glass. Heavy. Unhurried.

The fake housekeeper stepped through the shattered doorway, rifle raised, eyes sweeping the room like he had all the time in the world.

"Come out, Whitlock," he called, voice calm. "No use hiding."

I steadied the pistol I'd taken from the first man, breath shallow.

"Don't miss," I whispered to myself.

I fired.

He dropped with a howl, leg blooming red. His rifle hit the floor. I was up and moving before he could reach it. He clawed for a sidearm. Too slow. I put one in his head. Silence rushed in, heavy as the smoke. I covered the woman's body with a curtain torn from the window. It wasn't enough, but it was something.

I searched for the men quickly. Knives, ammo, cigarettes. No wallets. No ID. Professionals. Then the walkie-talkie crackled in the dead man's pocket.

"Night Eagle, report. Whitlock still in the room? Ambush is set."

My blood turned to ice. They were everywhere. I bolted out, grabbing a sheet from the housekeeping cart to cover the second body slumped inside. Another honest worker, throat slashed, eyes staring at nothing.

I ran.

Lily had the door cracked when I reached it. She saw my face, saw the blood on my shirt, and pulled Isaiah close.

"What happened?"

"No time." I grabbed her hand. "They found us. We are going now."

She didn't ask questions. She scooped Isaiah up, and we ran for the truck, the dawn just starting to bleed pale across the sky.

Death had been waiting in the quiet.

And it wasn't done with us yet.

I buried the gas pedal the second we hit pavement. The tires screamed as gravel exploded behind us, rattling the undercarriage like buckshot. The engine roared, wild and furious, vibrating through the seat and straight into my bones. My hands slipped on the wheel, slick with sweat, adrenaline surging so hard it made my vision pulse.

Lily crouched in the back seat with Isaiah crushed to her chest, rocking him as she whispered, "We're okay. We're okay."

I wanted to believe her.

Headlights flared in the rearview mirror. Two sets. Closing fast.

The first truck was a newer blue Ford, paint gleaming as it surged forward like a predator. The second was an ancient, rust-eaten monster from another age, rattling and smoking, with a mounted machine gun bolted crookedly into its bed. White hoods clung to the rails, sheets snapping in the wind, rifles already raised.

"Hold on!" I shouted.

Gunfire ripped the truck apart.

Bullets shattered the rear window in a storm of glass. Shards flew through the cab, stinging my neck and arms. Lily threw herself over Isaiah as rounds punched through the upholstery and tore into metal. The car screamed but kept running.

"We're hit!" she cried.

"Get down!" I yelled.

Shots ripped through the dash and doors, chewing holes inches from my head. Hot casings pinged off the trunk. By some miracle, none of it found flesh.

I yanked the pistol from under the seat and fired blindly out the window. The muzzle flash lit the cab white hot. Bullets sparked off steel, buying us a second. Only a second.

The blue Ford surged alongside us.

A Klansman hauled himself out of the passenger window and jumped.

The roof buckled under his weight. The car swerved hard, tires howling.

"Lily, take the wheel!"

"What?"

"Now!"

I shoved the pistol at her and climbed out the window as she scrambled forward and grabbed the wheel with both hands. The car fishtailed, then steadied. Wind tore at me as I hauled myself onto the roof.

The Klansman swung a club. I ducked the first blow. The second clipped my shoulder and sent fire racing down my arm. I tasted blood.

I punched him in the gut and felt the air rush out of him. Then his jaw. He grabbed my collar and yanked. My boot slipped. For a heartbeat, I hung over the edge, asphalt screaming beneath me.

I clawed back up and smashed my head into his face. Bone crunched. He reeled. One more punch sent him tumbling off the car and vanishing into the dark.

The Ford rammed us.

Metal screamed. The impact nearly tore me loose. Lily cried out, but kept us straight.

She raised the pistol and fired at their front tire.

The shot boomed.

Rubber shredded. The Ford spun, sparks and smoke pouring off it before it slammed into the ditch.

The old truck thundered closer.

The machine gun swung toward us.

I jumped.

My boots hit the wooden bed hard enough to rattle my teeth. The gunner turned, eyes wide behind his hood, swinging the barrel toward me. I grabbed it and shoved it skyward as he fired. Bullets ripped into the sky.

He punched my ribs. Pain exploded. I drove my elbow into his throat. He gagged and stumbled. I shoved him, and he went over the side, hitting the road with a sound I felt in my gut.

"You bastard!" the driver roared, grabbing a shotgun and twisting in his seat. Ducked behind the gun as he fired. Pellets are made of shredded air and wood.

Another engine pulled alongside.

Lily.

Our eyes met for a split second.

She fired.

The driver slumped forward, and the truck veered, smashing the guardrail and flipping nose-first into the ditch. Wood splintered. Metal crushed in a roar of violence.

I jumped clear just before it rolled.

The crippled Ford lurched back into view, Klansmen leaning out with rifles, faces twisted with rage.

I grabbed the machine gun and pulled the trigger.

The world shook.

The gun thundered, ripping the night apart. Bullets tore through steel and glass. The truck erupted in flames and skidded across the highway in a screaming ball of fire.

Then silence.

Fire crackled. My lungs burned.

Lily screeched to a stop. "Caleb! Get in!"

I dove into the car, shaking, blood-soaked, and gasping.

"You okay?" I asked.

She nodded through tears. "We're alive."

Isaiah lifted his head. "Did we win?"

I pulled them both close.

"For now."

Lily hit the gas, and the road vanished beneath us. Wreckage burned behind us, like ghosts in the dawn.

JESSE POV

Hours later, two vehicles crept down the desolate highway: a sheriff's cruiser and Jesse Boone's battered Ford. Smoke still rose in lazy curls from the twisted wreckage Caleb had left behind. Bullet casings gleamed in the dirt like scattered coins, mixed with shards of glass and dark, drying stains that spoke of violent ends. The air hung heavy with the acrid bite of gunpowder and burned rubber.

Jesse stepped out first, boots crunching on debris. Mary Beth Hollander followed, one hand pressed to her mouth as she surveyed the carnage: charred trucks crumpled like tin cans, bodies already zipped into bags by the deputies.

"This..." she breathed, voice trembling beneath forced calm, "this is impossible."

A county deputy approached, hat in hand, sweat beading on his forehead. "We handled it quietly, Jesse. Called it a bootlegger feud gone bad. Folks'll buy it. Nobody needs to know it was Klan business."

Jesse nodded once, sharply. "Good man. I knew you would."

Mary Beth couldn't tear her eyes away. Shock flickered across her face, quickly buried under colder calculation. Caleb had done this. Alone. Turned trained men into corpses and wreckage.

"He killed them all," she whispered, more to herself than anyone.

Jesse's jaw flexed. He stared at the smoldering remains, something raw flashing behind his eyes before he locked it down.

"Told you it wouldn't be easy," he said, voice low. "They're fighting for their lives now."

Mary Beth folded her arms tight, masking the tremor in her hands with steel. "Let them fight. Caleb humiliated me. Turned my name into a joke. And that girl... she stole what was mine. They'll pay for it. Slowly."

Jesse exhaled through his nose and turned back to his truck. He popped the trunk, pulled out a folded road map, and spread it across the warm hood. The paper crackled under his fingers.

Mary Beth watched him. "What are you doing?"

"Thinking," he said, tracing routes with a steady finger, eyes narrowed in concentration.

She frowned. "That doesn't explain anything."

Jesse's lips curved in a faint, humorless grin. "Doesn't have to."

He studied the web of highways, towns, and back roads, piecing it together like a puzzle only he could see. Where would Caleb run? Not south, too many eyes. Not east, too close to Klan strongholds. West meant open desert, nowhere to hide. North, then. Toward the bigger cities, where influence thinned and strangers blended in.

His finger stopped on a major junction leading to Dallas, then beyond.

"There," he said, tapping the map. "That's where he's headed. Big city. Fewer of our people. Thinks he can disappear in the crowds, start over where nobody knows his name or mine."

Mary Beth leaned closer. "You're sure?"

Jesse folded the map with precise snaps. "I know how he thinks. Better than anyone. He'll figure the farther north, the safer. Places where sheets don't mean power anymore."

He met her gaze, eyes sharp and confident. "And that's exactly where we'll be waiting."

Mary Beth's expression didn't change, but something hungry flickered in her eyes. Approval. Anticipation.

Jesse tossed the map onto the seat and climbed into the driver's seat. Mary Beth slid in beside him without a word.

The engine roared to life. Tires spun, kicking up dust and ash as they peeled out, following the same scarred highway Caleb had taken hours before.

The hunt was far from over.

And Jesse Boone, with his quiet cunning and unbreakable resolve, intended to end it on his terms.

CHAPTER FIFTEEN

The city swallowed us whole. Buildings rose so high they seemed to scrape the blue from the sky, brighter than anything back home. Neon signs blinked and buzzed even in daylight. Horns blared. People streamed past in every color and style imaginable. The air was thick with unfamiliar smells: hot dogs hissing on a street cart, exhaust, perfume, something that felt like freedom. Isaiah pressed his face to the window, eyes wide, mouth open, taking it all in.

"Look, Caleb! That sign's a giant boot, and it's kicking!" he shouted, pointing at a flashing cowboy boot swinging back and forth. "And that one's a chicken eating chicken! Lily, look!"

I couldn't stop the grin spreading across my face. His joy was so pure it pushed the shadows back, even if only for a moment. Lily laughed beside him, the sound soft and startled, as if she had forgotten that kind of joy was still hers.

We found a corner diner with chrome trim and red vinyl booths, the kind of place that still had two doors: one marked "WHITE" and the other "COLORED." Both opened into the same long room split by an invisible line no one dared cross.

Lily lifted Isaiah out of the car and smoothed his hair. "Come on, baby. Let's get some real food."

I followed them through the colored entrance. The second I stepped inside, the room went still. Forks paused halfway to mouths. Conversations died. Eyes turned not to Lily or Isaiah, but to me. A white boy in the wrong half.

A man at the counter stared like I was a ghost. A woman clutched her purse tighter. Someone muttered, "Lost, I reckon."

Heat crawled up my neck, but I kept my chin up and walked straight to the booth Lily chose.

To break the ice, Lily slipped a quarter into the jukebox and picked a song. Chuck Berry's guitar ripped through the speakers, bright and alive with "Johnny B. Goode." Isaiah's face lit up like Christmas.

"That's my song!" he yelled, jumping to his feet right there in the aisle. He started dancing, wild spins and hops, shoulders shaking, feet stomping like he could outrun every bad thing that had ever happened.

Lily laughed, full and free, the sound wrapping around my heart. Some folks smiled despite themselves. The tension eased, just a fraction.

The waitress approached slowly, pad in hand, voice careful. "Sir... there are seats open on the other side if you'd rather."

"No, ma'am," I said, meeting her eyes. "I'm right where I want to be."

She hesitated, then nodded with a small, knowing smile. "All right, then. What can I get y'all?"

Isaiah ordered chocolate-chip pancakes like they were treasure. Lily asked for eggs, bacon, grits, and a biscuit. I got steak and eggs, though food was the last thing on my mind.

Isaiah got a paper placemat and crayons and immediately started coloring a purple cow with wheels instead of legs. Lily leaned back in the booth, exhaling like she'd been holding her breath for days.

I just watched them.

The morning light slanted through the window, catching in Lily's hair, turning Isaiah's curls gold. His tongue poked out in concentration as he drew. Lily reached over and stole one of his crayons to add a sun to his picture, and he giggled when she made it wear sunglasses.

They were beautiful. Alive. Safe, for now.

My chest felt too full, like it might burst. This was what I'd been fighting for: moments like this. Isaiah's laughter rings over Chuck Berry. Lily's hand brushes mine across the table, casual and certain. The way she looked at me was not with fear or doubt, but with trust. With love.

I'd never had a family breakfast before. Not a real one. Not one where I belonged.

Back home, meals were tense, silent things ruled by my father's moods. But here, in this little colored section of a city diner, with syrup-sticky fingers and crayon masterpieces and Lily's smile warming me more than the coffee, I had it.

I had them.

And God, I was happy. Happier than I had any right to be after everything we'd lost, everything still chasing us.

But worry gnawed at the edges. Every laugh felt borrowed. Every glance toward the door reminded me they were still out there, Jesse, my father, men who wouldn't stop. I'd promised Henry I'd protect them. I'd promised myself.

Lily caught me staring again. She reached across and laced her fingers with mine, right there in the open.

"Hey," she said softly. "We're okay. Right now, we're okay."

Isaiah looked up, syrup on his chin. "Are we a family now?"

Lily and I looked at each other. No hesitation.

"Yeah, baby," she said, voice thick. "We are."

CHAPTER SIXTEEN

Jesse Boone drove with one hand loose on the wheel, the other tapping an uneven rhythm against the door, keeping time with the slow ache of an old Hank Williams song drifting from the radio. The road stretched ahead, dark and empty, headlights carving a narrow tunnel through the night.

Mary Beth Hollander sat angled toward the window, knees tucked close, blonde curls lifting and settling with each rise in the pavement. She hummed along without thinking at first, then let the words come, soft and unpolished, full of a sadness she did not bother to hide.

Jesse glanced at her, the corner of his mouth twitching. "You know every word."

She smiled faintly. "Daddy said a girl ought to learn the sad songs early. Life gives you plenty of reasons to use them."

"That's so."

"It was for church, too," she added. "Hymns on Sunday. Heartbreak the rest of the week."

Jesse chuckled, surprised by the sound of it. "You ever met a hymn that could keep up with you?"

She nudged his arm. "I behave when I want to."

They laughed together, quick and unguarded, the sound filling the cab before fading back into the hum of the engine. For a handful of miles, the weight between them lifted. They could have been younger then, untouched by choices and consequences, just two kids riding down a quiet road.

Mary Beth turned back to the window. Her reflection hovered faintly in the glass, eyes darker than they had been earlier.

"It's strange," she said softly. "How fast folks decide who you are without asking." She hesitated. "They look at me like I'm already finished. Like everything I worked for doesn't count anymore."

Jesse's tapping stopped. "They don't get to do that."

She breathed out, shaky. "Feels like they already have."

He kept his eyes on the road. "Only if you let them."

She studied him, searching his face in the dim dash light. "You really believe that."

"I know it," he said. Not loud. Not angry. Certain. "They don't own your name. Your future. None of it."

Her hands clenched in her lap. "I built my whole life to fit what they wanted."

Jesse nodded once. "Then it's time you took it back."

The words settled between them, heavier than comfort, sharper than sympathy. Mary Beth's breath caught. She looked away, blinking hard.

No one had said that to her. Not lately. Not when it mattered.

"Thank you," she said quietly.

He gave a short nod, jaw tight. "I mean it."

The radio rolled into another lonely song. The highway stretched on, pale lines slipping beneath the truck, the town behind them shrinking into nothing.

Mary Beth watched Jesse drive, the focus on him, the way he held the wheel as if it were the only thing keeping him steady. She recognized something there. Not love. Not yet. But alignment. A shared hunger for what had been denied.

They drove on in silence, no longer just running from what hurt them.

They were moving toward something they meant to reclaim.

CALEB POV

By the time Lily and I slipped deeper into the city, night had settled in fully, thick and soft as velvet. Neon signs buzzed overhead, their reds and blues bleeding across rain-dark pavement and pooling in shallow puddles like broken constellations. We moved with the crowd but not of it, shoulders close, Isaiah's small hand wrapped tight in mine. Every few steps, Lily's fingers brushed my arm, a quiet check-in, a reminder that we were still together, still standing.

The hotel sat a few blocks off the main drag. The Franklin. A narrow brick building squeezed between a pawn shop and a diner that had already gone dark. Half the sign had burned out long ago, leaving only FRAN glowing weakly in tired red, as if even the name was trying to disappear.

Inside, the lobby smelled of dust and old smoke. The wallpaper peeled at the corners, curling back like it had heard too many things and wanted no part of them anymore. The clerk was an older man with wire-rimmed glasses and a face that carried kindness without curiosity. He slid the key across the counter, then leaned in, lowering his voice.

"Barrow Street," he said. "Down the stairs. No sign. Mixed crowd. Folks just trying to breathe free for a while." He paused, studying us gently. "Might do you some good."

He winked, once. It was enough.

Our room was on the fourth floor, overlooking an alley so narrow that the buildings leaned toward each other, as if sharing secrets. The window rattled when trucks passed, the mattress sagged in the center, and the radiator hissed as if it resented company. But the door locked. The curtains closed. That was all we needed.

Isaiah fell asleep almost immediately. I pulled the thin blanket up to his chin and brushed the curls back from his forehead. In sleep, he looked untouched by fear or loss, like the world had not yet figured out how to hurt him. I stood there longer than I meant to, watching him breathe, then turned.

Lily stood at the window, arms folded around herself, city lights washing her face red, then blue, then red again.

"You wanna go see that place the clerk mentioned?" she asked quietly. "Just for a bit. Might be nice to feel... normal."

Normal felt like a foreign word. But I wanted it anyway. "Yeah," I said. "Let's go."

The club had no name, just a narrow staircase sinking beneath the street. Music pulsed through the concrete, a living thing you could feel before you heard. At the bottom, a heavy door opened into a cloud of smoke and a dim, red light.

A small band crowded the stage, horns, drums, and bass weaving together into something alive and swinging. The room was packed. Black and white faces mixed without hesitation. People laughed, danced, leaned close. Hands linked. Bodies moved like the rules aboveground had no authority here.

I stopped just inside the door. Not from fear. From awe.

Lily slid her hand into mine and squeezed. "See?" she said softly. "It ain't all broken."

We let the music take us. The faster songs came first, bright and driving. Lily laughed when I missed a step, bumped into me on purpose, and spun beneath my arm with a grin that felt like sunlight. Watching her move, loose and unguarded, something inside my chest eased for the first time in days.

Then the tempo slowed. The lights dimmed deeper red. The saxophone stretched a note so long and aching it seemed to pull the whole room closer.

Couples drifted together.

Lily stepped into me without asking, her arms sliding around my neck. My hands found her waist, natural as breath, and we swayed. No rush. No fear. Just the steady rhythm and the warmth of her body fitting against mine like it always had.

"You're wound tight," she murmured.

"Hard not to be."

"Then let me hold some of it," she said. "Just tonight."

I rested my cheek against her hair. The world narrowed to the sound of her breathing, the steady beat of her heart. For a few precious minutes, nothing chased us.

"You ever think," I whispered, "what it might've been like if we'd met somewhere like this?"

She tilted her head up, eyes catching the red light. "I think I'd have found you anywhere."

The words settled deep.

"I love you," I said quietly, like saying it too loud might break the moment.

Her smile trembled but held. "I know," she said. "And I'm still here."

I kissed her then, slow and sure, everything unspoken wrapped into it. Around us, the music carried on, the crowd moving as one living thing.

For that night, beneath the city, we were not running.

CHAPTER SEVENTEEN

By the time Lily and I slipped back into the hotel, the hallway had gone still. Only the radiator argued with the cold, rattling like it refused to surrender. The floorboards creaked under our steps, so we moved slowly, trading small smiles that still carried the warmth of the music we'd left behind.

I eased the key into the lock and pushed the door open. The room glowed faintly under the streetlamp outside, yellow light leaking through the thin curtains. Isaiah slept sprawled on his stomach, one arm thrown out, breath slow and even. Seeing him like that, safe and unaware, loosened something tight in my chest.

Lily came up beside me. "He didn't move," she whispered.

"Wore himself out," I said.

We closed the door softly and stood there a moment, letting the quiet settle. The night lingered on us, the echo of the club still humming under our skin. Lily's hair had come loose, soft around her shoulders, catching the light when she turned toward me. The look she gave me was gentle, steady.

She lifted her hand and brushed my jaw. "Are you scared?" She asked.

My heart was beating so fast, and my body was shaking with fear. "Never been more scared in my life, we have the whole world hunting us, and the scariest moment is also the best one."

She kissed me then slowly departed. "We will take it slow." She said.

She stepped closer, close enough to feel her warmth. Her hand slid to the back of my neck and drew me down. The kiss was slow, unguarded, like we were finally saying what we'd both been carrying. I held her at the waist, pulling her close, grounding myself in the feel of her. Everything I couldn't say poured into that moment.

We moved carefully, mindful of Isaiah only a few feet away, settling onto the edge of the bed. The mattress creaked, the radiator hissed, the city murmured beyond the walls. None of it mattered. Only Lily was there. The way her breath caught when I kissed her cheek. The way she whispered my name like it meant something sacred.

Lily's mouth traced along my jaw, my neck, her touch unhurried but sure. I buried my face in her hair, breathing her in, feeling the way she pressed closer as she trusted me to hold her together. Every movement felt deliberate, intimate, filled with everything we'd survived to get here.

The world narrowed to warmth and breath and the quiet rhythm we found together. Fear softened. The road fell away. There was only her, only this moment, only the shared certainty that we were still alive and still choosing each other.

After, we lay tangled beneath the thin covers, Lily resting against my chest, my arm wrapped around her. Isaiah slept on, unaware, safe. Lily traced slow circles against my skin, her breathing steady, content.

CHAPTER EIGHTEEN

Morning sunlight slanted across the city, glinting off cracked windows and dusty brick as Jesse Boone eased the Ford to the curb outside the rundown hotel. He killed the engine and stepped out, rolling his shoulders to shake off the ache of the all-night drive. Mary Beth climbed out beside him, smoothing the wrinkles from her dress with quick, precise movements. Exhaustion shadowed her eyes, but she held her chin high, every inch the unflappable Southern belle.

Across the street, six men waited in the mouth of a narrow alley, half-hidden in shadow. They weren't locals. Too still. Too watchful. Their clothes didn't match, but their eyes did, cold, flat, professional.

The leader stepped forward as Jesse approached, a tall man with slicked-back hair and a jaw so sharp it could cut glass.

"We picked up their trail leaving that club," he said, voice low. "They're holed up inside. Haven't come out. But we don't have the room number or floor."

Jesse absorbed it, mind already spinning angles. Too many rooms. Too many exits. Caleb was slippery, and time was bleeding away.

He turned to Mary Beth. "You're going in. Front desk. Sweet-talk the clerk. Get the room number, the floor, anything useful."

She nodded without hesitation, eyes lighting with something eager and dangerous. Jesse reached into the glove box and handed her a small pistol wrapped in cloth, along with a slim silencer.

"Just in case," he muttered.

She slipped them into her purse like they were compact and lipstick, then checked her reflection in the truck's side mirror, tucking a curl into place. With a practiced sway, she crossed the street and disappeared through the lobby doors.

Jesse and the assassins waited, tense in the shadows.

Inside, the lobby was dim and stale. The clerk, a wiry young man with a polite smile, looked up as Mary Beth approached.

"Excuse me, sugar," she said, voice honey-sweet, leaning just enough to draw his eye. She slid Caleb's photograph across the counter. "Have you seen this boy? It's essential."

The clerk glanced at the photo, then back at her, apologetic but firm. "Ma'am, I'm sorry. We can't give out guest information."

Mary Beth tilted her head, a smile softening into something almost playful. "You sure? Not even for a girl in distress?"

He offered a kind but unwavering smile. "I'm sure. And... I'm not into girls, if that's where this is going."

The words landed like a slap she hadn't seen coming. For one heartbeat, her perfect mask slipped. Shock. Then humiliation, hot and sudden. The clerk wasn't just refusing, he was dismissing her entirely.

Her smile froze, brittle at the edges.

From across the street, Jesse watched through the glass. He saw her pause. Saw her hand dip into her purse. Saw the shift in her posture, graceful turning lethal.

Mary Beth spun smoothly, pistol already raised, silencer gleaming.

Pfft.

The shot was no louder than a cough. The clerk dropped behind the counter, a neat red hole in his forehead.

She didn't flinch. Didn't look down. Just lowered the gun and waved Jesse in with a small, calm gesture, as if she'd done nothing more than sign a register.

Jesse burst through the doors, voice sharp. "Mary Beth, what the hell was that?"

She stepped over the body without breaking stride. "Plan changed."

Jesse bit back a curse and moved behind the counter, rifling through the registry book. His finger stopped on a fresh entry.

"Room 408. Fifth floor."

He looked up at the assassins. "Three elevators, three stairs. Quiet."

The men split without a word, melting into the building like smoke.

Mary Beth stood staring at the clerk's body, head tilted slightly, expression unreadable.

Jesse watched her, unease coiling in his gut. "You alright?"

She didn't answer right away. Then, softly, almost curious, "Am I supposed to feel something?"

Jesse didn't know what to say.

Because the truth was staring him in the face: Mary Beth Hollander wasn't shaken. Wasn't sorry.

She was empty.

And that made her more dangerous than any of them.

CALEB

I woke to sunlight slipping through the thin curtains, warm on my face, Lily's arm draped soft and heavy across my chest. For a few perfect seconds, everything was still. Her breathing slow against my shoulder, her hair tickling my neck, the faint scent of her skin filling the air. Peace. Real peace. The kind I'd never known could exist.

She stirred, eyes fluttering open, and a sleepy smile curved her lips. "Morning," she whispered, voice husky with sleep.

Before I could answer, she scooped the sheet around herself like a toga and slipped out of bed, laughing under her breath at her own makeshift dress. She padded to the bathroom, the door clicking shut behind her. A moment later, the shower hissed on.

I sat up slowly, smiling despite everything, and started gathering our scattered clothes from the night before. Isaiah slept on, dead to the world, one small foot sticking out from the blanket.

I should order breakfast. Please give us a little more time to get back to normal before we hit the road again.

I picked up the room phone and dialed the front desk. It rang twice before a cheerful voice answered.

"Front desk, how can I help you?"

"Yeah," I said, keeping my voice low so I wouldn't wake Isaiah. "Room 408. Could we get breakfast sent up? Eggs, bacon, pancakes for the kid, whatever you've got."

"Hang on just a second," the clerk said, sounding distracted. "Got someone walking in."

The line went muffled, as he'd turned away from the receiver. I heard footsteps, the squeak of the lobby door, then a woman's voice, clear and sharp.

"Excuse me, sugar. I'm looking for a guest. Caleb Whitlock?"

My blood turned to ice.

The clerk's voice came back, polite but firm. "Ma'am, I'm sorry, we can't give out guest information."

A beat of silence.

Then chaos exploded on the other end: a sharp intake of breath, the unmistakable whisper-soft puff of a silenced shot, a body hitting the floor. Jesse's voice roared through the line, raw with shock.

"Mary Beth, what the hell are you doing? That wasn't the plan!"

The phone slipped from my hand and clattered to the floor.

They were here.

I bolted for the bathroom, heart slamming against my ribs. Steam poured out as I shoved the door open. Lily jumped, clutching the sheet to her chest, eyes wide with alarm.

"Caleb? What—"

"Get dressed," I said, voice shaking. "Right now. They found us."

Her face went pale, but she didn't waste time asking questions. She dropped the sheet and grabbed her clothes, while I darted back into the room, yanking on my jeans and shirt and shoving my feet into boots.

Isaiah stirred, blinking sleepily. "Caleb?"

"Up, buddy," I said, forcing calm into my voice as I scooped him into my arms. "We're leaving. Quick and quiet."

Lily was already dressed, hair still damp, face set with that fierce determination I loved so much. She grabbed our small bag while I snatched the gun from under the pillow.

We had seconds.

I cracked the door, peeking into the hallway. Empty. For now.

The fragile peace of the morning shattered like glass.

They were coming.

And this time, we had nowhere left to run.

CHAPTER NINTEEN

The second I cracked the door, the elevator cables groaned high above, metal whining as the car climbed too fast. They were already in the building. Already close.

"Move," I hissed.

I eased the door shut and hurried Lily and Isaiah down the hall, slipping us into a narrow recess where a vending machine glowed weakly against the wall. It offered little protection, but it hid us from view. My heart pounded as I drew the revolver, thumb grazing the hammer, forcing my breath to stay quiet.

The elevator dinged. Doors slid open with a tired scrape. Three men spilled out, dark coats, quick eyes, moving like they'd done this a hundred times. They went straight to our room. One knocked sharply and cheerfully.

"Housekeeping!"

No answer.

The stairwell door banged open. Three more joined them. The leader, silver at his temples and jaw like granite, jerked his chin at the biggest.

"Kick it."

One brutal boot and the door exploded inward, wood splintering.

I raised the revolver, finger tightening. Lily's hand clamped my arm, eyes pleading. Isaiah pressed against her, shaking. The hallway was a kill box. One wrong shot and they'd be caught in the crossfire.

The men stormed the empty room, curses echoing.

I exhaled slowly. "Lily... take the gun."

"No." Her whisper cracked.

"Take it." I pressed it into her hand, closing her fingers around the grip. "I'll draw them off. You get Isaiah to the stairs. Don't stop."

She searched my face, tears brimming, but nodded once. Fierce.

I kissed her hard and fast. "Go when it gets loud."

I grabbed the fire axe from the wall mount and the extinguisher beside it. My hands shook, but I gripped tight.

"Lord, don't let me mess this up," I muttered.

Then I stepped into the open.

"HEY!" I bellowed.

Every head snapped toward me.

I swung the axe down onto the extinguisher with everything I had.

BOOM. HISSSSS.

The canister ruptured, screaming across the floor like a missile. A white chemical fog erupted everywhere, thick and choking, enveloping the hall in seconds. Gunshots cracked wildly, bullets punching walls and lights in frantic bursts. The fire alarm shrieked to life, adding piercing chaos.

I dove back behind cover as plaster rained down on me.

"Go!" I roared at Lily. "GO!"

Through the swirling cloud, I saw her silhouette grab Isaiah and sprint for the stairwell. The door banged open and shut.

Two assassins broke off, coughing and cursing, chasing the sound of her footsteps.

The fog thickened, Boots thundered past me, silhouettes ghosting through the chemical cloud. I broke the opposite direction, lungs burning, heart hammering so hard it felt loud enough to give me away.

I rounded the corner too fast.

My shoulder clipped a fallen light fixture. It toppled, sparks showering as it hit the carpet. For a breathless second, nothing happened.

Then the flame caught.

It ran fast, hungry, racing along the cheap carpet and up the peeling wallpaper. Smoke curled upward, black and oily, biting my eyes. Heat licked at my calves.

"Damn it," I hissed.

The fire alarm wailed louder, joined now by the angry crackle of burning insulation. The building groaned as if it were waking from a deep sleep. This was no longer just a distraction. It was a clock.

I heard shouting behind me. Orders barked sharply and angrily.

I ran.

The four assassins chased after me, ignoring the fire that was quickly building. I hid around the corner. The first assassin approached cautiously. He had his pistol raised, looking around. I tackled him low.

We crashed hard, his gun skittering away. He swung wildly. I drove my elbow into his throat. He gagged. I rolled off and kicked his temple. He went limp.

The second lunged with a knife. I blocked, steel biting deep into my forearm. Blood sprayed hot. I roared, grabbed his wrist, and slammed him face-first into the railing. Metal bent. He dropped the blade, clanging down the shaft.

The third fired point-blank. I twisted, a bullet grazing my side like fire. I charged, shoulder driving into his gut, lifting him off his feet, and smashing him against the wall. His breath exploded. I hammered his jaw until he slumped.

The fourth came silent, garrote wire flashing. It looped my neck before I saw him. Breath cut off. Vision blackened at the edges. I clawed back, nails digging skin, then threw myself backward. We slammed into the stairs. The wire loosened just enough.

I spun, elbow to his nose, knee to his groin. He doubled. I wrapped my arm around his throat and squeezed until he went slack.

Gasping, blood dripping from my arm, I snatched a fallen pistol.

JESSE POV

Meanwhile, deep inside the hotel, Jesse Boone felt something inside him fracture.

He had watched the plan unravel from the lobby, every silenced shot and shouted order turning to chaos. The smoke from the extinguisher still hung in the air, thick and choking, mixing with the sharp tang of blood and gunpowder. His men lay scattered, some groaning, some still. The clerk's body slumped behind the counter like a broken doll.

This was supposed to be clean. Quick. Quiet. A simple grab, a message sent, Caleb brought back into the fold or put down like a rabid dog. Instead, it was a slaughterhouse.

Jesse's hands shook as he reloaded his pistol, the metallic click too loud in the sudden hush. Caleb had done this. His Caleb. The boy he'd grown up with, fought beside, and trusted with his life. The brother he'd chosen.

And now Caleb was tearing through them like they were nothing.

Rage boiled up, hot and blinding, but beneath it lurked something worse: fear. Fear that Caleb had always been stronger, smarter, better. Fear that everything Jesse believed about loyalty, about blood, about right and wrong, was crumbling under the weight of what his best friend had become.

He couldn't let it end like this.

"This was supposed to be clean!" he roared, voice raw and echoing up the stairwell, carrying to every floor. "Quick! Quiet!"

A crash followed as he kicked over a fallen chair. The stairwell door slammed open. He was coming up.

Jesse took the stairs two at a time, pistol raised, boots pounding concrete. His breath came hard, not from exertion but from the storm inside him. He would find Caleb. He would end this himself.

No more hesitation. No more mercy. Caleb had made his choice. Now Jesse would make his.

MARY BETH POV

Mary Beth Hollander stood motionless in the lobby, her reflection faint in the glass doors as chaos unfolded beyond them. Through the haze of dust and flickering emergency lights, she watched the alley with unblinking eyes. She saw the assassin charge past the service door without a glance. She saw the faint scrape of the heavy door easing shut behind Lily and Isaiah.

She saw everything.

No scream rose in her throat. No cry for Jesse or the others. A cold clarity settled over her, sharp as the click of her heels would soon be.

Lily Jefferson thought she had escaped. Thought she had been clever.

Mary Beth's lips curved into a thin, humorless smile. She had been humiliated in front of the entire town, reduced to a punchline because of that girl, because Caleb had chosen her.

Not anymore.

She moved with deliberate calm, the revolver already in her hand as she pushed through the revolving door. The morning air hit her cool and crisp, but she barely felt it. Her heels struck the sidewalk in measured, predatory clicks as she slipped into the alley's mouth.

Lily was in there somewhere, hiding, thinking she was safe.

Mary Beth tightened her grip on the gun, eyes scanning the shadows, every sense tuned to the hunt.

This ended now.

On her terms.

LILY POV

The boiler room was a hell of rusted pipes and throbbing shadows, the air thick with heat and the low, menacing growl of ancient metal. Steam hissed from loose joints, and the dim bulbs overhead flickered like dying stars. Lily shoved Isaiah behind a massive boiler tank, pressing him low, her hand clamped over his mouth to silence his terrified whimpers.

The side door exploded open.

Mary Beth Hollander stepped through, heels striking concrete like gunshots. Her blonde curls caught the weak light, framing a face twisted with pure venom. The revolver in her hand gleamed steady and sure.

"I know you're here," she called, voice soft and singsong, laced with poison. "Come out now. Caleb can't save you."

Lily's heart thundered. She raised the gun, finger tight on the trigger, and fired.

The blast roared in the confined space. Mary Beth dove behind a water tank, her own shot answering a heartbeat later. Bullets sparked off iron, ricocheting in wild, screaming arcs. The air filled with the sharp bite of gunpowder and the scorch of metal. Isaiah screamed beneath her, high and piercing.

Mary Beth laughed, a low and cruel sound. "Brought the little one, did you? How precious."

Lily didn't wait. She charged.

They collided like opposing storms, slamming into a workbench. Tools clattered to the floor in a metallic rain. Mary Beth's nails raked Lily's arm, drawing blood. Lily drove her knee up, catching Mary Beth in the thigh. They staggered, locked together, breath hot and ragged.

"You stole everything!" Mary Beth hissed, shoving Lily back toward the roaring boilers. "My name. My future. My place!"

Lily slammed her elbow into Mary Beth's ribs, breaking her grip for a second. "I didn't steal anything! He chose!"

Mary Beth's eyes blazed. She swung wildly, fist cracking across Lily's cheek. Pain exploded white-hot. Lily's vision swam, but she shoved back, slamming Mary Beth against a pipe. Steam hissed around them, scalding the air.

"You don't deserve him!" Mary Beth snarled, fingers clawing for Lily's throat. "You're nothing!"

She pinned Lily against the scorching boiler, hands tightening, cutting off air. Lily choked, nails digging into Mary Beth's wrists, legs kicking for leverage.

Black spots danced at the edges of her vision.

Then a grinding screech cut through the chaos.

Isaiah.

The boy had crept to the massive steam valve on the far wall, small hands trembling as he seized the wheel. With a desperate cry, he twisted it with all his strength.

A violent groan ripped through the pipes. Then a deafening roar.

A jet of superheated steam erupted from the ruptured line above Mary Beth's head, blasting down like a dragon's breath. It missed her face by inches, scalding the air, searing skin, filling the room with blinding white vapor.

Mary Beth screamed, recoiling, hands flying to shield her eyes as the blast scorched the ground beside her.

"You little negro bastard," she shrieked, voice raw with pain and fury.

Lily seized the moment. She lunged, grabbing Isaiah and yanking him toward the narrow metal staircase in the corner.

"Run!" she shouted.

They scrambled up the steps, Isaiah's small legs pumping, Lily half-carrying him. Below, Mary Beth staggered through the choking steam, coughing, cursing, blinded but still deadly.

"LILY!" Her scream echoed through the pipes, inhuman with rage.

Lily slammed the upper door shut behind them and kept moving, pulling Isaiah through the hotel's lower corridors, heart pounding, lungs burning.

She didn't look back.

She couldn't afford to.

Caleb was out there somewhere, and she would find him.

No matter who stood in her way.

CALEB POV

Smoke clawed along the ceiling in thick, acrid tendrils, stinging my eyes and coating my throat with the bitter taste of burned chemicals and gunpowder. The building groaned and shuddered with every distant gunshot, vibrations rattling through the floorboards into my boots. My lungs burned from the effort, each breath ragged and hot, my hands slick with sweat and blood around the pistol grip. Pain throbbed in my back, my arm, my ribs, sharp reminders of every blow I'd taken, but all I could think of was Lily's face, Isaiah's small hand in hers. I had to reach them.

I hit the fourth-floor landing and rounded the corner.

Jesse stood at the far end of the smoke-choked hall, his silhouette sharp against the flickering emergency lights. The air between us hummed with tension, thick as the haze. Our eyes locked. Two boys who'd once shared stolen cigarettes and whispered dreams by the river now faced each other as killers in a burning hotel. The scent of scorched wood and cordite hung heavy, the distant wail of sirens just starting to pierce the chaos.

His pistol rose first, steady despite the tremor I knew was there.

I dove behind the splintered doorframe as bullets screamed past, slamming into the wall with explosive cracks. Wood shards exploded like shrapnel, peppering my skin with stinging bites. Plaster dust filled my mouth, gritty and choking. My ears rang from the thunderous blasts.

I scrambled low across the debris-strewn floor, glass crunching under my palms, and snatched a fallen assassin's gun still warm from his hand.

I fired back, the recoil jarring up my arm, muzzle flash lighting the hall in brutal white bursts. Jesse ducked behind cover, the shots echoing like thunder in the narrow space.

Standoff. Two shadows at opposite ends, smoke swirling thick and bitter, the air alive with the crackle of flames below and the metallic tang of blood.

I risked a glance toward the shattered window connecting the buildings. My heart seized.

Lily and Isaiah, covered in dust, faces pale with terror, running toward the gap. The sight of them alive hit me like a wave of pure relief, so intense my knees nearly buckled. They were close. So close.

Then Jesse's voice cut through the haze, low and raw, laced with pain that twisted like a knife.

"Why, Caleb?"

I froze, the words echoing in the smoke.

"Why betray your own kind? Your family? Why throw it all away... for some colored girl?"

The accusation hung heavy, bitter as the gunpowder on my tongue. I watched Lily pull Isaiah tighter, her eyes locked on mine across the divide, wide with fear but fierce with trust.

"Because I love her, Jesse," I said, voice steady despite the ache ripping through me. "She's the family I choose. The one worth fighting for."

Silence. Thick, suffocating, broken only by the distant roar of flames.

A sound came from Jesse's corner, soft, broken, almost a sob that tore at my chest.

"I was your family too," he whispered, voice cracking like thin ice.

The pain in those words hit harder than any bullet. For a heartbeat, I saw him again, the boy whom I'd saved from drowning, who'd had my back through every storm. My brother.

Then his voice hardened, cold and final.

"We could've had everything. But you threw me away."

I saw his hand move each down to the dead assassin beside him, fingers closing around the grenade on the man's belt.

"No—Jesse—"

He yanked the pin free, eyes blazing with fury and grief.

"I don't care anymore!" he roared, voice raw with agony. "I don't care!"

The grenade arced through the air, spinning end over end.

Time shattered.

Behind Lily, movement exploded from the shadows. The last assassin lunged, fist cracking across her face with a sickening thud. She crumpled to the floor, blood blooming at her lip. Isaiah screamed, high and piercing, the sound slicing straight through my heart.

The assassin leveled his pistol at her head, finger tightening on the trigger.

One bullet left.

The grenade spun closer.

I fired.

The round struck true. The grenade detonated mid-air in a blinding flash of white-hot light and deafening thunder. The shockwave slammed me backward, heat searing my skin like a furnace blast; debris rained down in a deadly storm of metal and fire.

I didn't think. I sprinted through the roar, boots pounding, and leaped through the shattered window. Glass tore at my arms and face in burning lines as I crashed into the next building, shoulder slamming tile hard enough to steal my breath and send pain exploding through my body.

I rolled and came up swinging.

The assassin loomed over Lily, pistol steady. I tackled him low and hard. We hit the floor in a tangle of fury and limbs. His gun skidded away with a clatter. He drove a knee into my ribs; agony bloomed white-hot, stealing my air. I tasted blood, copper-thick on my tongue.

He drew a knife, blade flashing cold in the firelight. I blocked the first slash, steel biting deep into my forearm, blood pouring hot and slick. He pressed closer, eyes empty and merciless, the blade inching toward my throat.

Lily, my fierce, unbreakable Lily, threw herself onto his back, nails raking bloody trails down his neck, fists pounding with desperate strength. "Get off him!" she screamed, voice raw with terror and rage.

He snarled, twisting to fling her away. The distraction broke his focus.

I seized the moment, grabbed the fallen knife, and drove it upward with every ounce of strength left in me. The blade sank deep. He gasped, a wet, choking sound, eyes widening in shock before he collapsed, lifeless.

Silence crashed in, broken only by our ragged, desperate breathing and Isaiah's heartbroken sobs.

Lily crawled to me, arms wrapping around my neck, pulling me close as tears streamed down her dust-streaked face. Isaiah buried himself against my chest, small body shaking with fear.

I held them both, tight as I dared, blood and sweat and tears mixing as the world burned behind us. The heat from the explosion still radiated through the walls, the air thick with smoke and the metallic tang of blood.

"We have to go," I rasped, voice hoarse.

We staggered to our feet and fled down the back hall, bursting into the alley as the building groaned and collapsed in a roar of flame and debris. Sirens wailed closer—fire trucks, police, the world descending.

Through the smoke at the front entrance, Jesse emerged, walking calmly amid the chaos, face etched with something hollow. Mary Beth appeared beside him, dress singed, eyes wild with unspent fury.

They climbed into the truck without a backward glance and drove away.

I pulled Lily and Isaiah deeper into the shadows, holding them close as the night swallowed us once more.

We vanished before the sirens could find us.

CHAPTER TWENTY

Night had fallen by the time Jesse and Mary Beth pulled into the gravel lot of a rundown motor inn just beyond the city limits. The neon VACANCY sign flickered erratically, casting a bruised red glow over the cracked asphalt. Jesse cut the engine and sat motionless, hands clenched around the steering wheel, knuckles white.

Mary Beth studied him in the dim light, her gaze steady and unreadable, sharp with something that went beyond desire, something possessive and raw.

"You did well back there," she said at last, her voice low and deliberate.

Jesse let out a hollow laugh. "Ezekiel won't see it that way."

"Ezekiel doesn't see what I see." She shifted closer, the seat creaking beneath her. "He doesn't understand what you're turning into."

Jesse turned his head, meeting her eyes. "And what's that?"

She reached out, fingertips brushing the tense muscle of his forearm. "A man who finishes what he starts. The only one with the spine to hunt Caleb Whitlock to the ends of the earth."

The words landed heavy in his chest, praise he wasn't used to, praise that felt like a drug. He swallowed, throat dry.

"I see it burning in you, Jesse Boone," she continued, voice dropping to a murmur. "Real strength. Real purpose. A fire nobody else has."

Silence stretched between them, thick and electric.

"And I want to stand in that fire with you."

Something inside him gave way, not tenderness, not romance, but a fierce, desperate need. For recognition. For alliance. For someone to match the rage eating him alive.

He reached for her first, pulling her across the console and into the backseat in a tangle of limbs and urgency. The door to their room was barely shut behind them before clothes hit the floor. There was no softness here, no slow exploration; hunger sharpened by betrayal and adrenaline. Her nails raked down his back as he pressed her against the wall, mouths clashing, teeth scraping. She arched into him with a low, guttural sound that wasn't surrender. It was a demand. He answered with the same ferocity, lifting her onto the dresser, then the bed, the cheap frame groaning under their rhythm. Every thrust carried the weight of what they'd lost, what they hated, what they still wanted to destroy. Her breath came hot against his neck, fingers twisted in his hair, pulling hard enough to hurt. It wasn't love; it was a shared vow, sealed in sweat and fury and the kind of release that left them both shaking.

Afterward, Jesse sat on the edge of the bed, shirtless, elbows on his knees, staring at the faded floral wallpaper as if it might offer absolution. Mary Beth lay propped on the pillows behind him, sheet pulled loosely to her waist, watching him with half-lidded eyes, satisfied, calculating, already planning the next move.

The phone on the nightstand rang, its shrill tone piercing the quiet room.

Jesse flinched.

Mary Beth's lips curved. "That'll be him."

Jesse snatched up the receiver. "Yeah."

"Boone." Ezekiel's voice rolled through the line like distant thunder, cold, clipped, barely containing rage. "You got any idea the mess you left me to clean up? Feds are crawling all over every chapter house from here to Richmond. Phones have been ringing nonstop since dawn. Do you care to explain yourself?"

Jesse straightened, gripping the receiver tighter. "I had Caleb cornered. Things escalated."

"Escalated?" Ezekiel's laugh was bitter, humorless. "You turned a downtown hotel into a goddamn war zone. Witnesses described armed white men fleeing the scene. Sirens for blocks. Highways are crawling with federal agents. That ain't escalation, boy. That's a catastrophe of biblical proportions."

Jesse closed his eyes. "We'll contain it."

"You'd better pray you can," Ezekiel snarled. "Because tonight the D.C. headquarters called an emergency council. Caleb Whitlock's name was the only one on every lip. He humiliated us. Exposed us. Made the whole organization look weak in front of God and everybody."

Mary Beth sat up slowly, sheet falling away, watching Jesse's face like she could read the conversation through his reactions.

Ezekiel's voice dropped, each word deliberate as a hammer strike. "So the Elders voted. Unanimous."

Jesse's blood turned to ice. "Voted on what?"

"As of this moment, Caleb Whitlock is number ten on the national bounty registry."

Jesse went perfectly still. The top ten wasn't just money. The top ten meant that every brother, every chapter, and every informant from Florida to the Pacific Northwest would have their description memorized. Eyes everywhere. No hiding.

"Number ten," Jesse echoed, voice hollow.

"You put him there, Boone," Ezekiel said, quieter now, laced with warning. "Don't make me regret backing you. Fix this. Bring him in or put him down. But do it clean next time."

The line clicked dead.

Jesse lowered the phone slowly, staring at nothing.

Mary Beth slid forward, wrapping her arms around him from behind, bare skin warm against his back. She rested her chin on his shoulder, lips brushing his ear.

"You hear that?" she whispered, voice velvet and venom. "You did it. You pushed him into the top ten. The whole organization's watching now, and they're watching you."

He didn't move, breathing shallow.

She pressed a slow kiss to the side of his neck. "You're the one they'll remember. The one who forced their hand. The prince of this hunt."

Jesse's jaw clenched.

"You'll get him," she murmured, fingers tracing the fresh scratches down his back. "And when you do, I want to be right there, watching him realize there's nowhere left to run."

Jesse finally nodded, a single, sharp motion.

CHAPTER TWENTY-ONE

We found an abandoned duplex on the ragged edge of the city, its windows boarded over, the porch sagging as if it had given up years ago. Inside smelled of mildew and old smoke, but the door locked, the roof didn't leak, and the kitchen sink coughed up cold water when I turned the tap. After the hotel, after the gunfire and the screaming and the blood, that felt like mercy.

Lily eased me down onto a couch that had lost most of its stuffing. Every breath pulled at cracked ribs; the gash on my forearm had soaked through the makeshift bandage and started crusting over. I bit down on the pain and managed something that might pass for a smile when Isaiah looked my way.

He hadn't spoken since we fled the Franklin. Not a single word. He sat cross-legged on the bare floorboards near the far wall, arms wrapped tight around his knees, staring at nothing. Too small, too quiet. I'd seen that stillness before, on kids dragged out of burning villages, on men who'd watched friends die and couldn't find their way back to words. Isaiah was only six. He shouldn't have to know that silence.

"Isaiah," I tried, keeping my voice soft. "You want some water?"

He didn't answer. Didn't even blink.

Lily knelt beside me with a chipped bowl of water and a torn strip of sheet. Her hands shook as she dipped the cloth, but she kept her face steady. She always did.

"Hold still," she whispered.

The rag stung when it touched the wound, but I stayed quiet. She worked carefully, wiping away dried blood, her fingers brushing my skin like she was checking I was still real. She needed the contact as much as I did.

"You don't have to do this alone," I said low enough that only she could hear.

She paused, just long enough for me to notice. "I'm fine, Caleb."

She wasn't. Her eyes were swollen, the whites threaded red, though she'd swear she hadn't cried. Every few seconds, her free hand found my shoulder, the side of my neck, the line of my jaw like she was mapping proof that I hadn't bled out in that hallway.

When the cut was as clean as we could manage, she stood and crossed to a dusty shelf where an old transistor radio sat crookedly. She twisted the knob. Static hissed, then cleared.

"...breaking news from downtown. Federal authorities have confirmed a deadly confrontation at the Franklin Hotel earlier this evening. Multiple fatalities reported, including at least eight dead. Sources describe automatic weapons fire and explosions that collapsed portions of the upper floors."

My stomach dropped.

Lily's hand froze on the dial.

"Witnesses report seeing armed individuals fleeing the scene. The FBI has taken the lead in the investigation, and, in a related development, the Department of Justice has opened a sweeping criminal inquiry into the activities of the Ku Klux Klan across several southern states. Officials say tonight's violence may be directly linked to ongoing Klan operations."

Lily's breath caught. She pressed her knuckles to her lips.

I closed my eyes and leaned my head back against the couch. Eight dead. They were already turning it into a massacre headline, the kind that brought federal heat down hard and fast. The Klan would feel the walls closing in on them. Cornered men do ugly things.

The announcer kept talking, voice clipped and urgent. "Sources in Washington indicate the inquiry could lead to racketeering charges and the seizure of assets. More as this story develops."

Lily clicked the radio off. The sudden silence felt heavier than the broadcast.

Isaiah curled tighter into himself, rocking slightly now.

Lily lowered herself beside me on the couch, moving slowly, like the floor might give way. "Caleb... this is bad."

"Yeah."

"They're not going to let it go. Not with the feds involved. Not now."

"No," I said. "They won't."

She looked toward Isaiah, then back at me, voice dropping to barely a whisper. "And Jesse... he'll take it personally. He already did."

I didn't answer. I didn't need to. We both knew what desperation would do to a man like Jesse Boone. He wouldn't wait for orders anymore. He'd come himself, and he wouldn't care who got caught in the crossfire.

Lily slipped her hand into mine. Her fingers were ice cold.

Hours later, Isaiah finally slept, curled under the one thin blanket we'd found, his breathing shallow but steady. Lily tucked it around him, smoothing the hair off his forehead with the kind of gentleness that made something ache deep in my chest.

When she was sure he was out, she came and sat beside me on the floor, back against the couch, shoulder touching mine.

For a long time, neither of us spoke. The old house creaked around us. Somewhere outside, a dog barked once and went quiet.

"We can't stay here," she said finally.

"I know."

But knowing and moving were two different things. My body felt like it had been run over, then backed up on for good measure. And every mile we put between us and the city meant another mile Isaiah had to endure this nightmare.

Lily rested her head against my good shoulder. "Where do we even go, Caleb?"

I stared into the dark, listening to the slight sound of Isaiah breathing.

"I don't know yet," I said. "But we'll figure it out. We always do."

"Caleb," Lily whispered, her voice barely carrying over the creak of the old house. "By morning, they'll have roadblocks on every way out. Checkpoints on the highways, eyes on the bus station, the train yard. We have to move. Tonight."

She was right. I knew the second the words left her mouth. But the tremor in her voice wasn't just about the Klan or the feds. It was about me, about the blood still seeping through my shirt, about the way I kept favoring my left side. She was terrified I wouldn't make it through another hour, let alone another day.

I rubbed my hand over my face. "And go where, Lily? Another city? Another abandoned house? We keep running until there's nowhere left?"

She looked down at her hands, knuckles white where they gripped the edge of the couch. "I don't know yet. But staying here means dying here."

Silence settled between us, thick and exhausting.

"We don't have money," she said finally. "Can't buy tickets. Can't even afford gas if we had a car." She lifted her eyes to mine, steady now, resolute. "So we take one."

I let out a slow breath. "Lily..."

"What choice do we have, Caleb?" Her voice sharpened, but not with anger but with desperation. "After everything they've done to us? After what happened at that hotel? Stealing a car is the least of the sins on anybody's ledger tonight."

I leaned my head back against the wall, feeling the rough plaster bite into my scalp. "It's not about right or wrong anymore. It's just... I spent years trying not to become the kind of man who does this."

She shifted closer, her shoulder pressing against mine. "You're not becoming anything. You're surviving. We all are." Her fingers found mine in the dark, calm and sure. "The man you were... he wouldn't have made it this far. And I wouldn't trade the man sitting here now for anything."

The words landed softly, but they cut deep. She meant them as comfort. Instead, they felt like confirmation: the old Caleb was gone, and whatever was left might not be worth saving.

I stared at the ceiling, cracks spidering through the plaster like fault lines. "Maybe we should split up," I heard myself say. "You and Isaiah could—"

"No." The single word cracked like a whip. She pulled back just enough to look me in the eye. "Don't you dare finish that sentence."

"I'm not saying I want it," I said quickly. "I'm saying... maybe it's safer. For you. For him."

Her expression softened, but only a fraction. "Safer? Caleb, the safest place either of us has been in weeks is right next to you. Please don't take that away from me. Please."

I swallowed hard. "Okay."

She studied my face for a long moment, making sure I meant it. Then she nodded once, decisive. "We leave tonight. North. As far as this car will take us. Away from their territory. Away from anyone who ever knew our names."

I squeezed her hand. "North it is."

Relief flickered across her face, fragile and fleeting. She brushed at her cheek with the back of her wrist, pretending the dampness there was nothing.

I pushed myself up, pain flaring hot through my ribs. At the cracked window, I paused, scanning the empty street below. A handful of cars sat along the curb, shadows in the weak glow of a distant streetlamp. Most looked old enough that hot-wiring wouldn't take much.

I didn't want to do this. But wanting had stopped mattering a long time ago.

"Stay with Isaiah," I said quietly. "Keep him calm. I'll be quick."

She stood too, catching my arm before I could move. "Caleb." Her voice dropped to almost nothing. "Come back to us."

"I will."

I leaned in and pressed my lips to her forehead, lingering just long enough to feel her tremble. Then I slipped down the stairs, moving slowly, testing each step so the old wood wouldn't betray me.

Outside, the night air is crisp and clean. I kept to the shadows, eyes sweeping the street for any sign of movement. None came.

The third car down was a faded blue Chevy with a dented fender and Virginia plates. Door unlocked. People still trusted too much in neighborhoods like this.

I slid behind the wheel, the vinyl seat cracked and cold. My fingers found the panel under the dash, stripping wires with muscle memory I wished I didn't have. A spark, a twist, and the engine coughed, caught, and settled into a low rumble.

I eased the car forward without headlights, pulling into the mouth of the alley beside the duplex. There, in the upper window, I could make out Lily's silhouette watching. She didn't wave. She didn't need to.

I left the engine running and waited, one hand on the wheel, ready to load up the only two people left in the world who still believed I was worth saving.

We were leaving this city behind tonight. Whatever came next, we'd face it together.

CHAPTER TWENTY-TWO

Morning filtered through the faded motel curtains, a weak blade of gray light slicing across the threadbare carpet. The room carried the stale ghosts of countless cigarettes and cheap cleaner, the kind of scent that clung to places charging three dollars a night just off the highway. Jesse sat hunched over the rickety table by the window, a police scanner crackling beside him, its green glow flickering across a state map spread flat beneath his palms.

The portable radio on the dresser murmured low, the announcer's voice thin and distant.

"Authorities continue to investigate last night's deadly incident at the Franklin Hotel. Sources confirm a stolen vehicle may be linked to suspects still at large."

Jesse's jaw clenched hard enough to ache. His fingers pressed white against the map's edges. Every report about that car felt like salt ground into an open wound.

He leaned closer to the scanner, straining for anything useful amid the routine patrol chatter. Nothing yet.

Mary Beth emerged from the bathroom, her damp hair still wrapped in a towel. She wore one of his white shirts, sleeves rolled high, hem brushing her thighs. Barefoot, she crossed the room and settled her hands on his shoulders, thumbs digging into the knots of muscle.

"You're strung tighter than fence wire," she said softly, working the tension with slow circles.

He didn't respond. Didn't look up. His gaze stayed locked on the map, tracing highways and back roads like they were veins leading straight to Caleb.

She bent and brushed her lips against his cheek, lingering there. Even that barely reached him.

"Jesse," she tried again, voice lighter, "why not just sweep the city block by block?"

"He's not in the city anymore," he muttered.

She stilled her hands. "How can you be so sure?"

"Because I know him." Jesse finally leaned back, scrubbing a palm over his unshaven face. "Better than he knows himself. We grew up together. Fought together. Spent every damn summer fishing Red Creek until the sun burned us red. Got our backsides whipped by the same belt more times than I can count." A faint, bitter smile ghosted across his mouth and vanished. "I know how he thinks."

Mary Beth slipped into the chair across from him, studying the storm in his eyes. This wasn't the cold duty of a Klansman on assignment. It was something rawer, something that had been festering for years.

"This isn't about the Klan, is it?" she asked quietly. "Or him running off with that girl."

Jesse went rigid for a heartbeat. Then he shook his head once. "No. It's personal." His voice scraped like gravel. "He didn't just turn his back on them. He turned his back on me."

The radio hissed into static, filling the heavy silence.

Jesse stared at the map as if it might burn. "To hell with the Klan," he said, lower, harder. "I want him dead for what he did to me. I'll chase him to the grave if that's what it takes."

Mary Beth's breath caught. She rose slowly, crossed the short distance between them, and kissed him fiercely and intensely, fingers threading into his hair, pulling him into her as she could feed on the rage itself. When she drew back, her eyes gleamed with sudden clarity.

"Then let me give you something," she whispered against his mouth. "A real lead."

He lifted a brow.

She leaned over the table, tapping a red nail on the map. "Call the county clerk's office. Ask about any property old man Jefferson owned up in Texas. Something rural. Forgotten. The kind of place Caleb might figure no one would ever think to look."

The idea struck him like a bolt from the blue. Jesse surged to his feet, chair scraping loudly against the floor. He snatched the rotary phone off the wall and dialed with quick, sure spins.

"Damn," he muttered as it rang. "Why the hell didn't I see that before?"

The line clicked. A voice answered on the other end.

Jesse's eyes went cold and sharp, every inch the hunter finally catching the scent.

CALEB POV

The sun was only a pale smear on the horizon when we eased onto the highway, the stolen Chevy groaning with every shift of the gears. I kept her under sixty, afraid the old engine might shred itself if I asked for more. In the rearview mirror, the city faded into a hazy smudge, thin columns of smoke still rising from the wreckage of the Franklin Hotel. Each mile felt like it was being stolen, like we were borrowing time we had no right to.

Lily sat beside me, arms folded tight across her chest, staring out at the endless stretch of frostbitten fields. In the back, Isaiah lay curled beneath the thin blanket we'd taken from the duplex, eyes open but fixed on nothing. He hadn't truly spoken since the hotel. A few whispers, maybe, but nothing that reached us. I kept checking the mirror, waiting for some small sign: a question, a complaint, even tears. Silence was all he gave.

"The road's clear," I said, to hear something besides the engine. "No one behind us. No patrols."

Lily nodded, but her gaze stayed on the window. Her fingers drummed a restless beat against her thigh.

"We can't keep driving with no destination," she said at last, voice low. "Anywhere with people is a risk. Jesse won't stop at the city limits. He'll spread out. He always does."

I opened my mouth to answer, but a small voice drifted up from the backseat.

"...the farm."

My foot eased off the gas. I glanced in the mirror. Isaiah had pushed himself upright, blanket clutched in both fists, eyes fixed on the road ahead.

"What farm, bud?" I asked, gentle as I could.

"Daddy's old one," he said, the words raspy from disuse but clear. "The one he bought a long time ago. We only went once."

Lily's breath caught. She pressed a hand to her mouth. "Oh God. I'd forgotten it even existed."

I looked at her. "You own a farm?"

She shook her head slowly. "Not really. Daddy bought the land after the previous owner died. Said the soil was rich, that he'd fix up the house one day and rent it out." Her voice wavered. "He never got around to it. We drove out there once, walked the property, and left. The house is falling apart. No one's been near it in years."

"Where?" I asked.

"About an hour north of here," she said. "Past Pine Hollow. You take a dirt track off the county road. Nothing else around for miles."

A long breath left my lungs, half relief, half dread. "That might be exactly what we need."

Lily turned to me, eyebrows drawn together. "You think it's safe?"

"No neighbors," I said. "No traffic. No reason for anyone to go looking." I glanced back at Isaiah. "He needs quiet. We all do."

She studied my face for a moment, then gave a slight nod. "All right."

I reached over and covered her hand with mine. She turned it palm-up and laced our fingers together, a simple grip that said more than words could carry right then.

"Thank you, Mr. Jefferson," I murmured under my breath, too low for anyone else to hear. "I'm still trying."

Lily squeezed once, steady and warm.

"Tell me how to get there," I said.

She leaned forward, peering through the windshield. "Stay on this road for now. In a few miles, you'll see a faded sign for Pine Hollow. We turn left just past it."

Isaiah settled back against the seat, head resting on the window. His eyes were still open, but something in them had softened. He wasn't fixed, not even close, but he'd spoken. He'd pointed us somewhere. That was enough to keep the wheel steady.

I pressed the accelerator a little harder; the Chevy rattled in protest but held together.

We were heading toward the one place in Texas no one should think to look for us.

For the first time in days, the road ahead seemed to lead somewhere worth reaching.

The sun hung low as we rolled up the rutted drive to the old Jefferson farm, a bruised orange disk bleeding light across the horizon, too tired to climb any higher. The place looked forsaken even by time itself. Knee-high weeds, brittle and golden, choked the yard. The house leaned heavily to one side, porch steps rotted through, and windows stared out like empty sockets. But it was quiet. Ultimately, quiet felt like a gift of grace.

Isaiah was out of the car before I killed the engine. He bolted across the field, small legs churning, dust rising in his wake. I leaned against the warm hood and watched him run, a dark silhouette cutting through the tall grass, as if the open space could scrub the hotel from his skin.

Then he stopped dead, bent down, and pulled something from the dirt: a faded red blanket, frayed at the corners, left behind by some long-gone field hand. He shook it out, draped it around his neck, and knotted the ends beneath his chin.

And just like that, he was Superman.

He took off again, arms spread wide, the makeshift cape flapping behind him as he made whooshing sounds only he could hear. Laughter spilled out of him, bright and startling in the stillness. I felt it hit me square in the chest, warm and unexpected, spreading until I was smiling without meaning to.

"He needed this," Lily said softly at my side.

I hadn't heard her approach. She slipped her arm through mine and rested her head against my shoulder. Her breathing slowed, matching the easy rhythm of the evening. Watching Isaiah play did something to her I hadn't seen in days; it loosened the fear knotted around her heart. It loosened mine, too.

For the first time since the world caught fire, Isaiah wasn't afraid. He was simply a boy with a cape and a field big enough to hold every dream he still had left.

Lily's fingers tightened on my arm. I covered her hand with mine. In that small moment, under a dying sun, we looked like something whole. Something worth protecting. I let myself believe it, just for a breath. Maybe this forgotten place could hide us long enough for the storm to pass. Perhaps I could keep them safe for real this time.

But another part of me, the part that had learned caution the hard way, knew better. Jesse wasn't finished. The Klan wasn't finished. The world rarely grants quiet to people like us without demanding payment later.

Still, I held Lily close and watched Isaiah race the fading light, his laughter carrying across the empty field, and I let the warmth stay anyway.

Night folded over the farm like a thick, unyielding quilt. Wind slipped through gaps in the walls, making the old house creak and sigh. Moonlight spilled through holes in the roof, laying pale stripes across the dusty floorboards.

Isaiah slept hard on a mattress we'd dragged into the corner, curled tight inside his red blanket like it could shield him from everything. His thumb rested against his lips, chest rising in the deep, even pulls of a child finally too exhausted to fight sleep.

I watched him for a long minute, just to be sure he was still breathing. Still here.

Lily sat beside me on the sagging couch, knees drawn to her chest, chin resting on them. She had kept moving since we arrived: sweeping dirt, boarding a broken window, checking on Isaiah again and again. Anything to keep her hands busy and her mind from catching up.

Finally, she spoke, voice so low I barely caught it. "Caleb... I lost everything."

She stared straight ahead, eyes shining in the dim light, fingers twisting together.

"My home is gone. I don't even know if there's anything left of it. Mama's gone. Daddy's gone." Her voice cracked, raw and small. "The only things I have in this world are you and Isaiah."

Tears slipped down her cheeks faster than she could wipe them away.

"I'm scared," she whispered. "I try not to be. I try so hard. But I'm terrified. Terrified of losing you both. Terrified of waking up one day and you're not here. Terrified of dying out here in the middle of nowhere. Terrified of... everything."

The words broke loose then, and so did she. Sobs tore out of her, harsh and ragged, everything she had buried since the night her father died, since the hotel, since the running began. She folded forward, hands covering her face, shoulders shaking.

I pulled her into my arms. She collapsed against me as her bones had finally given out. I held her tight, one hand stroking her back, murmuring soft nonsense into her hair. The words didn't mean much, but she clung to them anyway, fists bunched in my shirt.

Slowly, the storm inside her quieted. Her breathing evened. Her grip loosened, but she didn't let go.

"I'm right here," I whispered. "I'm not going anywhere."

She didn't answer. Exhaustion took her before she could. Her head stayed heavy against my chest, fingers still curled weakly into the fabric of my shirt, as if loosening them might make me vanish.

I kept holding her long after my own eyes burned. Sleep crept in quietly, pulling me under while the old house settled around us, guarding what little we had left for one more night.

CALEB'S DREAM

Darkness swallowed everything first. Heavy. Absolute. Suffocating. Then the torches flared to life one by one. Dozens of them. Dozens of white hoods emerged from the black, circling tighter, their robes flickering orange in the dancing light. Shadows writhed across the ground like living things, reaching out with inky fingers that clawed at my boots.

I turned in a frantic circle and saw Jesse standing there. Ezekiel is right beside him. Both men watched me with eyes that held no mercy. Both smiled with the same cold, empty smile, their teeth gleaming unnaturally white in the firelight.

A scream shattered the night.

Lily.

My heart seized.

She hung tied to a rough wooden cross, arms wrenched high above her head, bare feet dangling inches from the dirt. Her hair fell wild across her face. She struggled to speak, to call my name, but another raw scream tore from her throat and swallowed the words.

Ezekiel stepped close. He pressed something heavy into my hand. A torch. Its end is already wrapped in oil-soaked cloth, dripping and ready.

"Light it up, boy," he said, voice calm as a judge passed a sentence. "Finish what you started."

I tried to drop it. Tried to hurl it away. My arm refused. My fingers closed tighter around the shaft, traitors to my own will, knuckles cracking from the strain.

I looked at Lily. "No," I whispered. "No. Please, no."

But my feet moved forward on their own, dragging through the mud like they were chained to invisible weights. The torch lowered. The flames kissed the dry wood piled at the base of the cross.

Fire exploded upward in a hungry roar, heat blasting my face like the breath of hell itself.

Lily's scream became something beyond human, a sound that clawed straight into my soul, ripping at memories and regrets. The blaze caught her clothes, her hair, racing over her skin in bright, merciless waves. Flesh blistered and blackened before my eyes, peeling away in charred strips that fell like ash snow.

Through the curtain of flame, she lifted her head. What had been her eyes now burned with living fire, sockets glowing like embers in a forge. Then she laughed. A deep, guttural rasp that belonged to no person I knew. It echoed inside my skull, ancient and unforgiving, multiplying until it filled the air from every direction.

"It's all your fault," she said, the voice scraping out like gravel and smoke, layered with echoes of every voice I had ever failed—my mother's, Mr. Jefferson's, even my own.

"You promised."

Her charred hand reached through the flames toward me, fingers curling as if to pull me in, bones cracking audibly as the heat warped them into hooks. The circle of hoods began to chant, low and rhythmic, words I couldn't make out but felt in my bones, vibrating through the ground. Jesse stepped closer, his smile widening into a grin that split his face too far, revealing rows of sharpened teeth.

"You did this," he hissed, voice blending with the flames' crackle. "You lit the match. Now watch her burn."

Lily's body twisted in the fire, not in agony but in transformation. Her skin sloughed off completely, revealing muscle and bone beneath, still writhing, still alive. The flames leaped higher, forming shapes of the dead from the hotel, mouths open in silent accusation, eyes fixed on me.

Isaiah appeared suddenly at her feet, small and untouched by the blaze, looking up at me with wide, betrayed eyes. "Why didn't you save us?" he asked, voice innocent and piercing.

I reached for him, but the torch in my hand ignited my own sleeve, fire crawling up my arm, searing flesh without pain, just the cold certainty of guilt. Lily's laugh grew louder, swallowing the chant, the screams, everything, until it was the only sound left in the world.

"You promised," she repeated, her burning form leaning forward, the cross creaking as it bent toward me. "And promises burn hottest of all."

Her hand closed around my throat, pulling me into the inferno, the heat finally registering as endless, consuming agony.

Waking

I bolted upright with a sharp gasp, sweat soaking my shirt, chest heaving as my heart pounded wildly against my ribs. My hands trembled uncontrollably. Breath came in ragged bursts I couldn't calm. The room lay in near-total darkness, broken only by a thin blade of moonlight slicing across the warped floorboards.

Lily slept beside me, curled trustingly against my arm, her breathing soft and even. Peaceful. Alive.

I dragged a shaking hand across my face and fought the panic clawing up my throat. Just a dream. Nothing more.

But it didn't feel like only a dream. It felt like a warning carved into my bones, a reminder that the promises I had made were slipping further out of reach with every passing hour. Time was running out, and deep down I knew the fire was still coming.

CHAPTER TWENTY-THREE

Jesse's truck growled up the rutted dirt drive, headlights carving pale tunnels through the early morning mist. A convoy of dark, windowless vehicles trailed close behind, engines rumbling in perfect unison, each one loaded with men who had come to end this once and for all.

The instant Jesse cut the engine, the doors flew open down the line. Boots thudded onto the ground. From the bed of the rearmost truck, a lean assassin dropped down with a heavy duffel slung over his shoulder. He yanked the zipper and started pulling out weapons, sleek matte-black rifles handed off one by one without a word.

Jesse caught his mid-air, grip sure and familiar. Mary Beth took hers with both hands, the weight pulling her arms down for a fraction of a second before she steadied herself, jaw set with grim resolve. All around them came the sharp metallic chorus of magazines slamming home, bolts racking, safeties clicking off.

The men formed a precise firing line facing the sagging farmhouse, shadows stretching long in the weak dawn light. The assassin raised one hand.

"Ready."

Jesse dipped his chin once.

A storm of gunfire tore loose.

Muzzles flashed bright as sheet lightning. Bullets hammered the old house without mercy, ripping through weathered siding, punching out every window in sprays of glass, chewing the porch to splinters. Wood exploded outward in choking clouds. The whole structure shuddered and groaned under the onslaught, each impact a thunderous declaration that mercy had run out.

When the last magazine ran dry, silence crashed back in, heavy and absolute, broken only by the faint ticking of hot barrels cooling in the chill air.

Jesse stepped forward through drifting smoke, eyes narrowed on the ruined facade.

"Spread out," he said, voice low and edged with steel. "Surround it. Anything that moves dies."

The line dissolved instantly. Men fanned out in practiced pairs, moving fast and low, weapons trained on every shadow and doorway.

CALEB POV

I sat in the dim hush of the room, listening to them breathe. Isaiah lay curled on the thin mattress, his small chest rising and falling in a steady, rhythmic motion. Lily had tucked herself against his side, one arm draped protectively over him. For one fragile moment, everything felt still. Almost peaceful. The kind of quiet I had nearly forgotten could exist. Outside, dawn painted a faint orange line across the fields, soft and promising.

Then the world shattered.

Gunfire tore through the walls in a deafening roar. Bullets punched holes clean through the wood, showering us with splinters. I moved without thinking, yanking Lily down with me as we hit the floor hard. She woke gasping, eyes wide and confused, while shards of the house rained around us. I scrambled to Isaiah and threw my body over his just as another volley chewed the walls to pieces. He came awake with a sharp, terrified cry.

"Caleb!" Lily shouted over the thunder. "What is happening?"

"They found us," I said, voice low and grim.

Her breath hitched, a sound of fear that went straight to the marrow.

The shooting stopped as abruptly as it began. Silence rushed in, heavy and wrong. I knew what came next. They were reloading. Repositioning. Spreading out. Old Klan tactics Jesse and I had drilled together as boys. A bitter thing to share.

I checked my pistol. One magazine left. Nothing more.

"Perfect," I muttered.

I pointed to the narrow closet in the far corner. "Both of you. Inside. Don't move. Don't make a sound unless it's me coming for you."

They didn't argue. Isaiah scrambled into Lily's arms. She pulled the door open just wide enough, slipped them both through, and eased it shut with a soft click.

I moved.

I sprinted toward the back hall as the front door creaked open. A masked man stepped inside, rifle already raised. I fired once. Center mass. He dropped without a sound.

The men behind him opened up instantly.

I dove behind the kitchen counter. Wood exploded above my head, chunks flying. I waited, counting shots, listening for the pause. When their magazines ran dry, I surged forward.

The first man barely registered me before I drove into him, using his body as a shield against the next. My knee cracked his ribs. An elbow to another's throat dropped him, choking. They kept coming, pouring through the door.

I retreated until walls boxed me in on both sides. One leveled his pistol at my face. I kicked his wrist hard; the weapon spun upward. Before it hit the floor, I slammed an elbow back into the man behind me and felt his nose shatter. I hooked another by the neck, planted my boot on the sink, and launched myself upward. The height let me twist mid-air, tightening my grip until his neck snapped with a sickening pop.

His body fell. I caught the falling pistol, spun, and fired point-blank into the chest of the next attacker. He crumpled.

The last man in the kitchen charged, kicking the pistol from my hands. It clattered away. Fine. I met him fist for fist. He was fast, trained, and landed a solid blow to my jaw. I tasted blood but answered with a headbutt that staggered him. We crashed together, trading brutal strikes until I drove him back onto the old table. Wood splintered beneath him. He kicked wildly, heel clipping my chin, but I held on, locking my arm around his throat and twisting until he went limp.

I staggered back, lungs burning, the kitchen thick with gun smoke and blood.

No time to breathe.

I bolted for the back door, slipped on spilled blood, caught the frame, and burst into the yard just as more boots thundered across the porch.

I dove behind the rusted water trough and watched Jesse step calmly into the ruined kitchen, surveying the bodies with slow satisfaction.

"Caleb!" he called, voice carrying that old drawl laced with venom. "You can't hide forever, brother."

He wasn't talking to me.

He was listening to them.

My stomach knotted as he moved deeper into the house, pausing outside the closet door. Through the shattered window, I saw Lily's shadow pull Isaiah tighter, both frozen in silence.

Jesse reached for the handle.

No.

I sprinted for the barn, kicked the side door hard enough to rattle the hinges, grabbed a rusted bucket, and hurled it across the space. Metal clanged loudly against beams, echoing like a gunshot across the yard.

Jesse froze. Then turned.

He stormed out of the house, face twisted with rage, boots pounding straight for the barn.

I melted back into the shadows, pulse roaring in my ears.

I didn't wait to see him cross the threshold. I broke from cover and ran for the cornfield behind the barn, rows of dead stalks stretching tall and brittle under the rising sun. Gunfire cracked behind me. I dove between the rows as bullets shredded leaves overhead, showering me with fragments.

"Fan out!" Jesse bellowed. "Drive him deeper!"

Boots crashed in after me.

I dropped low, moving silently now, letting them charge past. One rushed too close. I yanked him down and drove my knife between his ribs. He gurgled once and stilled.

Another passed to my right. I hooked his ankle. He hit the dirt hard. My forearm crushed his windpipe before he could cry out.

A third crept forward, rifle sweeping. I rose behind him like a shadow, arm snaking around his neck, and twisted until bone gave way.

Three down.

Silence fell, thick and dangerous.

Then Jesse laughed, low and cruel from the edge of the field.

"Nice try, Caleb."

My blood turned to ice.

I pushed through the stalks and saw him standing at the boundary, a lighter already open in his hand.

"No," I breathed.

He flicked it. Flame danced. He tossed it into the dry rows.

Fire erupted with a hungry whoosh, racing along the ground faster than any man could run. Flames leaped from stalk to stalk, devouring everything in bright, roaring waves.

"Run, brother!" Jesse shouted over the crackle. "Let's see if the Lord wants you alive more than I do!"

Heat slammed into me. Smoke clawed my lungs. I turned and bolted deeper into the burning maze, leaping rows as fire chased at my heels. Corn popped and hissed, stalks collapsing in walls of orange. Every breath scorched my throat. The world narrowed to flame and smoke and the thunder of my own heart.

I slapped burning embers from my sleeves, coughing hard, eyes streaming. The blaze closed in from both sides, herding me forward into thicker, hotter air.

I was unsure if there was any end to the field anymore.

I only knew stopping meant dying.

Lily and Isaiah were waiting.

So, I lowered my shoulder and ran straight into the inferno, praying for any strip of ground that was not yet on fire.

CHAPTER TWENTY-FOUR

Mary Beth watched Jesse charge into the cornfield after Caleb, the two men swallowed quickly by the tall, brittle stalks. Distant gunshots echoed, sharp and erratic, but none found their target. The remaining men spread out, barking clipped orders, weapons sweeping the horizon. Mary Beth had no interest in waiting any longer.

She tightened her grip on the rifle and strode back toward the house, boots grinding against the parched earth. The screen door banged shut behind her as she stepped inside.

"Lily?" she called, voice laced with mockery. "Are you still here, sweetheart?"

She moved down the narrow hallway, trailing the rifle barrel along the flaking wallpaper, scraping paint with deliberate slowness. In the living room, she paused, eyes scanning every corner, every shadow.

She stopped at the closet door. A faint rustle. A held breath.

Her lips curved into a cold smile. She reached for the knob.

Inside, Lily's pulse thundered in her ears. She pressed a trembling finger to Isaiah's lips and braced her shoulder against the door.

Mary Beth's fingers closed around the handle.

Lily exploded outward.

The door swung wide and slammed into Mary Beth as Lily tackled her full force. The rifle spun from her grasp and clattered across the floor. Both women hit the ground hard, rolling in a tangle of limbs. Lily straddled her first, raining down punches with desperate fury.

Mary Beth blocked the third blow, bucked her hips, and flipped them. She pinned Lily beneath her and struck back viciously, fists hammering face and shoulders, teeth bared in a snarl.

Lily absorbed the hits, then drove an elbow deep into Mary Beth's ribs. Air burst from the woman's lungs. She toppled sideways with a grunt.

They scrambled upright at the exact moment and collided again, clutching arms, shoving, and straining like wild animals staking territory. Boots scraped across worn linoleum as the fight spilled into the kitchen.

Lily's fingers brushed cold iron. She seized the old cast-iron skillet from the counter and swung it in a vast, desperate arc. Metal met skull with a resounding clang. Mary Beth dropped like a stone.

She did not stay down.

Mary Beth swept Lily's legs. Lily crashed onto her back, breath knocked from her lungs. In an instant, Mary Beth was on her knees, pinning arms, hands clamping around Lily's throat.

Lily choked, nails raking at the iron grip. Her vision blurred red. Legs kicked uselessly against the floor.

Isaiah stood framed in the doorway, small face pale with terror.

"Lily?" he whispered.

Mary Beth ignored him, thumbs pressing harder.

Lily's face darkened to purple.

"Stop!" Isaiah screamed. He threw himself at her back, tiny fists pounding her shoulder. Mary Beth flung him away with one brutal shove.

He hit the floor hard, tears spilling. Then his eyes locked on the rifle lying just inside the doorway. He crawled to it, wrapped both shaking hands around the stock, and dragged the heavy weapon up.

He turned, chest heaving, tears streaking his cheeks.

"Get off my sister," he said, voice small but unwavering.

Mary Beth glanced back.

Isaiah pulled the trigger.

The shot roared through the small kitchen. Mary Beth jerked violently as the bullet struck her chest. She collapsed sideways, eyes vast and empty, blood pooling fast beneath her.

Outside, Jesse heard a single gunshot. He abandoned the field and sprinted for the house.

He burst through the door and froze.

Mary Beth lay motionless on the floor, blood spreading dark across the linoleum. A raw, broken sound tore from his throat. He dropped to his knees beside her, fingers brushing her cheek as if touch alone could bring her back.

"No," he rasped. "Mary Beth... no."

His gaze lifted slowly to Isaiah, the boy still clutching the rifle, barrel trembling.

Grief twisted into something savage. Jesse drew his pistol with a shaking hand and aimed it at the child.

"You little bastard—"

Lily launched herself at his arm. Her weight knocked the barrel downward. The gun discharged with a deafening crack. The bullet ricocheted off the stove and punched into Isaiah's side.

Isaiah screamed and crumpled, blood blooming fast through his shirt.

Lily shrieked his name and fell beside him, pressing both hands to the wound, trying to stem the flood.

Jesse staggered back, face drained of color. Horror flooded his eyes. He stared at the boy, at the blood on his own hands, at what he had just done.

For one endless second, he stood frozen, torn between rage and a guilt that threatened to swallow him whole.

Then he turned and fled, boots pounding across the porch, sprinting for his truck as if the devil himself were at his heels.

CALEB POV

I burst out of the burning cornfield, smoke pouring from my clothes. My chest heaved with each breath, every inhale burning like fire in my lungs. I stumbled forward, wiping ash from my eyes just in time to see Jesse sprinting across the dirt toward his truck. He climbed in and tore off down the road like a man fleeing hell itself.

"What the—?"

Then I heard it. A scream. High. Broken. Full of pain.

"ISAIAH!!!"

Lily.

I didn't hesitate. I ran, ignoring the burning in my lungs, ignoring the pain stabbing deep into my ribs, until I reached the doorway of the farmhouse. I stepped inside. And I stopped cold.

Lily was kneeling on the floor, her arms wrapped around Isaiah's limp, bleeding body. Her hands were slick with crimson. Isaiah's eyes fluttered weakly, barely holding on. Lily sobbed as she rocked him. "I-Isaiah... stay with me, baby... please stay with me..."

My heart shattered inside my chest. I had failed. My promise to Henry Jefferson was broken. Everything I swore to protect was bleeding in Lily's arms.

I dropped to my knees beside them, my hands trembling so badly I could hardly hold myself up.

"Oh God... oh God, no..."

The world around me blurred until nothing existed but the boy, the blood soaking into Lily's clothes, and the unbearable truth pressing down on me like a weight I could not escape. I was not fast enough. I was not strong enough. I was not enough. Not when it mattered most.

CHAPTER TWENTY-FIVE

The truck skidded wildly into the hospital lot, tires howling against asphalt as I slammed the brakes. I barely registered the crooked parking before I threw the door open and bolted, Isaiah cradled limp and bleeding in my arms. Lily stumbled out right behind me, both of us reeking of smoke and blood, our clothes stained dark.

"Help!" I roared. "Somebody help!"

Nurses and doctors swarmed us. Hands reached out, lifting Isaiah from my grip with urgent efficiency. Voices shouted orders. Wheels rattled as they rushed him through the swinging doors and out of sight.

Then everything stopped.

I collapsed into a plastic chair beside Lily in the waiting room, my hands still slick with his blood. The world hummed around us with ringing phones, hurried footsteps, distant beeps, but inside me, there was only a hollow void.

I stared at my trembling fingers, crimson drying under my nails. "This is my fault," I whispered, the words scraping raw from my throat.

Lily turned, face streaked with ash and tears. "Caleb, no—"

"I failed." My voice cracked like thin ice. "I failed your father. I failed you both. I swore I would keep Isaiah safe. I looked him in the eyes and promised." Tears burned hot, blurring everything. "I should have gone to the police from the start. Should have done anything but drag you into my war."

She reached for me, voice shaking. "We're alive because of you."

I shook my head, the guilt crushing my chest until breathing hurt. "Alive? Look at him. Look at what my choices did. I could outrun the Klan alone. Thought I could shield you." My fists clenched, nails biting skin. "But I'm poisoned. Everything I touch ends up bleeding."

She had no answer. The silence between us screamed the truth louder than words ever could.

A doctor entered then, face weary but kind. Lily surged to her feet. "Is he...?"

"We've stabilized him," the doctor said gently. "The bullet missed vital organs. He's a tough kid. He'll pull through."

Relief broke over Lily like a wave. She sobbed, clutching the doctor for a moment before turning back to me, eyes shining with desperate hope.

But I was already gone.

I slipped to the pay phone in the corner, hands shaking so violently I barely fed the quarter into the slot. The receiver felt cold against my ear. I dialed.

"Federal Bureau of Investigation."

"There's a man named Jesse Boone," I said, voice low, steady only by force of will. "He's hunting a woman and her young son. He's armed, dangerous, and part of a militia. They need protection. Now."

"Sir, your name?"

"It doesn't matter." I glanced back at Lily, her fragile smile fading as she realized the seat beside her was empty. "Just protect Lily Jefferson and Isaiah Jefferson. Please."

"Sir, stay on the—"

I let the receiver drop, cord swaying like a hanged man.

I walked back to her. She wiped tears, forcing a weak smile. "Caleb... he's going to be okay."

"I'm glad," I managed, voice barely above a whisper.

She reached for me. "Come sit."

I pulled her into my arms instead, holding her so tightly I felt her heartbeat against mine. She melted into me for one heartbreaking second.

"Caleb?" she murmured against my chest. "What's wrong?"

"I love you," I said, the words tearing free like a confession. "More than anything in this world."

She pulled back, brow creasing with worry. "Caleb...?"

"I need the bathroom," I lied, forcing calm into my voice. "I'll be right back."

She searched my face, then nodded, relief softening her features. "Okay. Hurry."

I memorized her in that moment: the ash on her cheek, the hope flickering in her eyes, the trust she still gave so freely.

Then I turned away.

I walked toward the restrooms but veered right at the hallway split, drawn inexorably toward the red EXIT sign glowing like judgment at the corridor's end. Each step felt heavier, like walking deeper underwater.

The door pushed open into the cold night air, sharp with coming rain. Hospital lights cast long, clawing shadows across the lot.

I paused just outside, chest aching so fiercely I nearly doubled over. Lily's voice echoed in my head, soft and pleading. Isaiah's small hand is trusting in mine.

God, I wanted to stay.

But staying meant death for both of them. Jesse did not want reconciliation. He wanted me. And he would burn everything to ash until he had me.

So, I gave him the only bait left, myself.

I crossed the lot to the assassin's truck, still idling where we had left it. I climbed in, shut the door with a quiet click that felt final.

The engine growled as I pulled away, headlights cutting a lonely path into the darkness. The hospital shrank in the rearview until its lights vanished.

Somewhere out there, Jesse was running too, wounded, raging, unraveling.

Good.

I tightened my grip on the wheel until my knuckles blanched white.

"He took everything from me," I whispered into the empty cab. "From all of us."

The road stretched black and endless ahead.

I pressed the accelerator harder.

I would not stop until Jesse Boone was dead.

CHAPTER TWENTY-SIX

Lily sat alone beneath the harsh fluorescent lights of the waiting room, the buzzing of the lights resembling distant insects. Her eyes stayed fixed on the hallway Caleb had disappeared down, willing him to reappear: a familiar stride, that quiet half-smile, anything. She checked the clock again and again, each passing minute carving deeper into her chest.

He was gone too long.

Far too long.

A cold dread coiled tight in her stomach, twisting harder with every second. She rose halfway from the chair, heart pounding, when the sliding doors hissed open.

Two men in dark suits strode in, movements precise and urgent. Federal agents. She knew it before they even spoke a word.

"Ma'am," the taller one said, badge flashing gold under the lights. "Lily Jefferson?"

She could only nod, throat closing.

"I am Agent Carter. This is Agent Ruiz. You and your brother are under federal protection, starting now."

The words struck her like ice water.

Caleb's phone call. His sudden excuse about the bathroom. The way he had held her so fiercely, like he was memorizing her.

He left.

He left us.

The realization crashed over her, sharp and suffocating. Anger surged first, hot and blinding. How could he? After everything they had endured together, after every promise whispered in the dark, after the way he had become her anchor, her home. How dare he decide for them? How dare he walk away without a goodbye?

She wanted to scream. Wanted to run after him and drag him back.

But the rage ebbed as quickly as it rose, draining into something far more devastating.

He had not left because his love had faltered.

He had left because it hadn't.

He left because he believed he was the danger, the poison drawing death to their door. He went to give them a chance at life without him.

A trembling breath escaped her. She lowered her head, tears burning tracks down her cheeks.

"I forgive you, Caleb," she whispered to the empty air, voice breaking. "Just come back to me. Please, God, come back alive."

CHAPTER TWENTY-SEVEN

Jesse Boone shoved through the warped door of the Klan clubhouse, the hinges groaning like an old accusation. Inside, the air hung thick with stale sweat, cigarette smoke, and the sour rot of defeat. A handful of men hunched over cards in the corner, voices forced loud, laughter brittle, all of them pretending the walls were not closing in.

Jesse did not spare them a glance. His boots dragged across the filthy floorboards as if each step carried the weight of a coffin. He collapsed into a rickety chair against the back wall, slumped forward, elbows on knees, and buried his face in trembling hands. Everything inside him ached with a sharper pain than any wound he had ever taken.

Mary Beth.

The name alone was a blade twisting in his gut. Her face flashed behind his eyes: the fierce spark in her gaze when she believed in him, the warmth of her fingers on his neck, the hungry press of her mouth promising they would burn the world together.

And then the final image: her body crumpled on that kitchen floor, eyes empty, blood pooling dark and accusing.

A choked sound escaped him, half sob, half snarl. Tears stung hot, spilling over before he could stop them. He did not bother wiping them away. Let the others stare. Let them whisper. Nothing mattered now.

A young Klansman approached without a word and set a glass of whiskey in front of him. Jesse grabbed it like a lifeline and threw it back in one savage gulp. The liquor scorched down his throat, raw and punishing, but it was nothing compared to the inferno already raging inside his chest.

The wall phone rang, shrill and insistent. Once. Twice. Three times.

No one moved.

Jesse exhaled a ragged breath that sounded like a sigh of surrender and hauled himself up. Whatever fresh hell waited on the line could not hurt worse than the one he already carried.

"Yeah?" he rasped into the receiver.

Ezekiel's voice exploded through the earpiece, thunderous and barely leashed. "Jesse. The feds are all over that farmhouse."

Jesse's grip tightened until his knuckles blanched.

"They found her," Ezekiel snarled. "Mary Beth. Found the boys you took out there. The place is swarming with agents. Are you hearing me, boy? You are a federal fugitive now. Your face is on every wanted poster from here to Washington."

The word fugitive struck like a hammer to the skull.

"Ezekiel, I can explain—"

"Explain?" Ezekiel roared, voice cracking with fury and something darker. "You dragged that girl into your blood feud! Mary Beth was innocent. She had a life ahead of her, a family, a future. And you snuffed it out in some godforsaken field because you could not let go of your damn pride!"

Jesse's jaw locked so hard it throbbed. "Caleb betrayed us. Betrayed me. I had to—"

"You had to do nothing!" Ezekiel's shout shook the line. "You failed. You brought the whole damn government down on our heads. We are done covering for you."

For the first time in his life, Jesse heard real fear in Ezekiel's voice. Fear of him.

The line clicked dead.

Jesse stared at the receiver, chest heaving, rage, and grief colliding until he could not tell where one ended and the other began. Slowly, he hung it up, the click unnaturally loud in the silent room.

He had nothing left. No brotherhood. No woman. No redemption. Nothing but a single, searing obsession that consumed every shattered piece of him.

Caleb Whitlock.

Jesse dragged the back of his hand across his wet eyes, the salt stinging like acid. He poured another whiskey with shaking fingers, stared into the amber liquid for a long heartbeat, then downed it in one burning swallow.

It tasted like the death of the teen he had been.

EZEKIEL POV

Ezekiel Whitlock lowered the receiver with deliberate care, as if the plastic might shatter under the weight of what he had just done. His jaw clenched so hard the muscles jumped. For a long, silent moment, he stared at the photograph on his desk: him, his wife, and a young Caleb, all three caught mid-laugh, their faces bathed in bright sunlight, untouched by the poison that would come later.

The image burned hotter than any rage he had ever felt.

This had spiraled beyond redemption. Beyond excuses. And now the mess fell to him alone to end.

His hand moved to the phone again, steady despite the fury roaring through his veins. When the line clicked open, his voice came out low and iron-cold.

"It's Whitlock. I need a problem handled. Quiet. Permanent."

No names. No explanations. Just clipped commands that left no room for misunderstanding. The man on the other end understood perfectly and agreed without hesitation.

Ezekiel set the receiver down and leaned back in his chair. His gaze returned to the photograph, lingering on his son's innocent smile.

"This is the only way," he whispered to the empty room, voice rough with something that might have been regret if he had allowed it to surface.

CHAPTER TWENTY-EIGHT

The whiskey seared a jagged path down Jesse's throat, but it did nothing to dull the ache gnawing at his insides. He stared at the scarred bar top, eyes unfocused, seeing only Mary Beth's lifeless face, Ezekiel's contempt, the smoking ruin of everything he had touched. The clubhouse murmured around him, low, nervous voices, cigarette smoke drifting like ghosts under the yellow lights.

Then the world died.

Every bulb snapped off at once. The jukebox choked mid-wail and fell silent. Darkness swallowed the whole room, thick and absolute. For one heartbeat, no one moved. Then came the confused curses.

"What the—"

Jesse's blood turned to ice.

Through the grimy window, he saw the streetlights across the road still burning steadily and calmly. Only this building had gone dark. Only them.

His glass slipped from his fingers and shattered on the floor.

"No," he whispered, voice cracking. "No... It is him."

He did not need to say the name. Every man in the room felt it settle over them like a shroud.

"Guns!" Jesse roared, the word ripping out of him raw and desperate. "Get your freaking guns, now!"

Chairs crashed backward. Boots pounded across the floorboards. Rifles were yanked from behind the bar, shotguns ripped from wall racks, shells clacked into chambers with frantic, shaking hands. Men scrambled to windows and doorways, silhouettes against the faint glow from outside, breathing hard, eyes wide with something close to terror.

Jesse lunged for the wall phone, snatched the receiver, and pressed it to his ear.

Dead.

No dial tone. Just cold, final silence.

The line had been cut.

He stood frozen in the blackness, heart slamming against his ribs so violently he thought it might burst. This was not the FBI with their warrants and floodlights. This was not Ezekiel sending discipline.

This was vengeance walking up the road in the dark.

This was Caleb, alone, silent, and done running.

Jesse's breath came shallow and fast. Sweat beaded on his forehead despite the chill creeping through the room.

He had hunted Caleb across half the state, burned fields, spilled blood, and taken everything. Now Caleb had come to collect, and the night itself held its breath, waiting for the first shot.

CALEB POV

I melted into the shadows behind the clubhouse, every sense razor-sharp, breath slow and silent. A lone Klansman stepped out the side door, flicking on a cheap flashlight that cut a feeble arc through the night. He swept it lazily between the buildings, muttering under his breath.

Nothing.

He never saw me.

He wandered closer to the power box, bending low to inspect the severed cables I had left dangling like gutted snakes. "What the hell...?"

I was struck.

My arm snaked around his throat from behind, choking off his cry before it began. I drove him face-first into the dirt, knee digging between his shoulder blades. One sharp, merciless blow to the temple. He went limp without a sound.

I stripped his rifle, checked the magazine, slung it over my shoulder, and ghosted to the back door. The knob turned with a faint, betraying creak as I eased it open. A narrow metal staircase rose ahead, swallowed by darkness.

Then hell erupted.

BOOM.

A shotgun roared inches from my face, the muzzle flash blinding, the heat searing a line across my cheek like a brand. Pellets shredded the doorframe where my head had been a heartbeat earlier. I dove sideways, shoulder slamming the wall as I rolled behind cover.

I snapped off three quick shots up the stairs, the muzzle flashes strobing the dark. No return fire. Just heavy, waiting silence.

Then the movement.

A figure descended slowly, shotgun cradled like he owned the night. No light. Pure arrogance.

I pressed deeper into the shadow, muscles coiled, breath held to nothing.

He hit the bottom step, head turning just enough.

I fired once. Center mass.

He crumpled without a word, body tumbling down the last few stairs in a heap.

I surged upward, clearing the first floor fast, then the second.

The door at the top exploded open.

He filled the frame like a wall of muscle and hate: the massive assassin from the hotel, the one I thought I had buried in that burning field.

My blood ran cold.

"I thought you died," I growled.

He grinned, teeth flashing white in the dark. "You killed my brothers. Tonight, I return the favor."

He charged.

His fist came like a sledgehammer. It caught me square in the ribs, lifting me off my feet and hurling me backward. Pain detonated through my side, white-hot and blinding. Before I could recover, he was on me, an iron grip twisting my shirt, slamming me into the railing hard enough to bend metal. My spine screamed. He drove a knee into my gut, folding me in half.

I clawed for my rifle. He kicked it away, the weapon clattering down the stairs into darkness.

Then he hoisted me overhead like I was nothing, arms straining, veins bulging. I saw the drop behind him, the long fall down the stairwell yawning open.

Not like this.

I twisted hard, slamming my knee into his chest, throwing my weight sideways. Momentum flipped. Suddenly, he was the one off-balance, eyes widening for a fraction of a second.

We fell together.

He hit the landing below with a bone-crushing impact, the sound wet and final. He lay still, neck twisted at the wrong angle.

I dragged myself upright, ribs grinding, blood filling my mouth, and forced my legs up the next flight.

Third floor.

Two Klansmen burst through the door at once, no guns, just raw size and fury. The first swung a haymaker that clipped my jaw and snapped my head sideways. The second tackled me low, driving me into the wall hard enough to crack plaster.

The world tilted. Blood flooded my mouth. For one dizzy second, I was back in the cornfield, fire closing in, everything slipping away.

No.

I roared inside, pure refusal.

I caught the first man's arm mid-swing, twisted until something popped, then drove my elbow into his throat. He gagged, staggering back. The second hammered fists into my sides, each blowing a thunderclap against cracked ribs. I absorbed it, let the pain fuel me, then pivoted and slammed my forehead into his nose. Cartilage crunched. He howled.

It dissolved into savage chaos: fists, knees, elbows, bodies crashing against walls and railings. They were large, well-trained, and brutal. I was faster, meaner, running on nothing but vengeance and the faces of everyone they had taken from me.

I broke one man's arm against the railing and felt the bone snap like dry wood. The other wrapped his hands around my throat, squeezing until black spots danced in my vision. I kneed him in the groin, then again, harder. His grip loosened just enough. I ripped free and drove my fist into his temple until he dropped, eyes rolling back.

They hit the floor and stayed there.

I did not wait to see if they would rise.

I staggered up the final flight, blood dripping from my split lip, ribs screaming with every breath, vision tunneling.

Top floor. Jesse Boone was up there, and I was done running away.

CHAPTER TWENTY-NINE

I heard the faint click of Jesse slamming the panic button a split second before the alarm pierced the air, a shrill, buzzing wail that vibrated through the concrete walls like a dying animal's scream. Heavy footsteps pounded overhead, frantic and uneven, echoing down the stairwell. He was scrambling, desperate, cornered in a way I had never seen him before.

I exploded up the final flight of stairs, boots slamming metal risers, lungs scorching with every ragged inhale. I burst onto the landing just as he charged through the doorframe, shotgun clutched in white-knuckled hands, barrel gleaming dull under the emergency red glow.

"There you are," he snarled, voice cracking with raw fury and something deeper, something broken.

The blast detonated like thunder in the confined space; the muzzle flash was blindingly white-hot, and acrid gunpowder smoke flooded my nostrils and stung my eyes. I hurled myself to the cold concrete, gravel biting into my palms as the slug screamed past my ear, so close I felt the rush of displaced air scorch my skin. Shards of shattered wall exploded outward, peppering my back like needles.

I fired back on instinct, the recoil jolting through my aching ribs, bullets chewing into the doorframe in bursts of splintered wood and dust. Jesse darts behind the corner, cursing under his breath, the air thick with the metallic tang of cordite.

He did not wait for me to recover. He bolted upward, boots hammering the stairs in a frantic rhythm, his breath coming in harsh, labored gasps that echoed off the walls. I pursued, chest heaving, fire, ears ringing with a high-pitched whine that drowned out everything but the pounding of my own heart. The stairwell reeked of sweat and fear, the cold metal railing slick under my grip.

He shoved through the roof door with a grunt, the hinge screaming in protest as frigid night air rushed in, whipping my face with icy needles. I followed, bursting out into the open darkness, the gravel rooftop crunching underfoot like broken glass.

He was waiting, coiled like a predator.

He lunged from the shadows with a feral roar, swinging the shotgun like a club. The stock slammed into my shoulder with bone-jarring force, pain erupting white-hot through my arm, nerves screaming as if branded. I hit the gravel hard, the impact driving the breath from my lungs in a guttural wheeze, sharp stones digging into my back through my shirt.

The shotgun skittered away across the roof, metal scraping tar with a grating screech.

Jesse kicked it over the edge without a glance, the weapon clattering down into the abyss below. "No guns," he panted, chest heaving, eyes wild and gleaming in the faint city glow. "Not for this. Just us."

I pushed myself up slowly, shaking the numbness from my throbbing arm, the night air biting cold against the sweat-soaked fabric clinging to my skin. I tossed my pistol aside; it bounced once and slid to the edge, teetering before vanishing into the dark. "Fine," I rasped, voice raw from smoke and exertion. "Let's end it."

His face contorted, not with pure hatred, but with a twisted agony, betrayal carved deep into every line, eyes glistening with unshed tears that caught the distant streetlights. "You should have stayed gone, Caleb," he said, voice trembling on the edge of a sob. "You were my brother. My only family."

I stepped forward, the gravel shifting under my boots with a low crunch. "I still am."

He let out a hoarse, shattered sound, half laugh, half wail, which echoed across the empty rooftop like a ghost's lament. Then he charged with a guttural yell, barreling into me like a freight train, his heavier frame crushing the air from my chest as we slammed down together. My back hit the gravel again, stones grinding into my spine, pain lancing up my ribs like shattered glass.

His fists rained down in savage arcs, knuckles splitting my lip on the first blow, blood flooding my mouth hot and coppery. I blocked the second, the impact jarring my forearms, but the third cracked against my cheekbone, stars exploding in my vision, skin splitting with a wet sting. I tasted salt and iron, felt warmth trickle down my face.

I bucked upward, knee driving into his thigh with a meaty thud, muscle giving way under the force. He grunted, grip loosening just enough for me to roll free, gravel embedding in my palms as I pushed to my feet. I wiped blood from my mouth with the back of my hand, the metallic taste lingering, breath coming in sharp gasps that fogged the cold air.

We circled each other slowly, boots scraping rough circles in the tar, the wind howling between us like a mournful witness. Below, distant dogs barked in a frantic chorus, car tires hissed on wet pavement, the city thrumming indifferent to the wreckage of two lives unraveling on this forgotten height.

"You chose them over me!" Jesse rasped, voice breaking, spittle flying from his lips, face twisted in anguish.

"There was no choice, Jesse," I shot back, the words tasting like ash. "You chose hate. You walked into this nightmare with your eyes wide open, and you dragged everyone down with you."

He roared and rushed again, faster than his size should allow. I sidestepped, but he clipped my side, sending fresh agony through my bruised ribs. I caught his arm mid-swing, twisted hard, and drove my elbow into his midsection with a dull thump. Air burst from his lungs in a wheeze, ribs compressing under the blow. He swung back wildly, knuckles grazing my jaw with a glancing sting that snapped my head sideways.

We grappled then, locked in a brutal embrace, chests heaving against each other, hot breaths mingling in the cold, his reeking of whiskey and despair, mine of smoke and blood. Boots slid and scraped across the rooftop, gravel flying up in gritty sprays. His fingers dug into my shoulders like claws, nails breaking skin, while I twisted his collar, choking him just enough to feel his pulse thunder under my grip.

"We were brothers, Caleb," he gasped against my ear, voice thick with tears, hot and ragged. "Nobody gave a damn about us back then. We had nothing but each other. Nothing!"

"We could have kept it that way," I choked out, throat tight with the weight of old memories, riverbanks, shared secrets, the boy who had been my only light in a dark childhood. "You didn't have to become this monster."

"I had to belong!" he bellowed, voice cracking like thunder. "You had your father, your principles. I had nothing but rage, Caleb. Nothing but this!"

His forehead smashed into mine with a sickening crack, bone meeting bone in a flash of blinding white pain that split my skull like lightning. Stars burst across my vision, blood trickling warm from my brow. I staggered back, boot heel catching the roof's edge, the void yawning below a dizzying drop to concrete oblivion.

Jesse saw it and lunged with a triumphant snarl, hands shoving at my chest to send me over.

I grabbed his coat in a desperate twist, yanking him with me. We teetered on the brink, gravel crumbling under our weight, the wind whipping our hair as the city lights blurred far below. At the last second, I pulled us both inward; we crashed down together in a tangle of limbs, gravel embedding in skin, well exploding in grunts of pain.

I wrestled free first, rolling to my knees and driving a fist into his ribs once, twice, three times, each blow landing with a meaty thud that forced wheezes from his lips, blood flecking his chin. His grip weakened, body shuddering under the assault.

But he surged up with one final, feral burst, knocking me backward with a shoulder charge that rattled my teeth. He grabbed my shirtfront and slammed me into the rusted frame of the water tower, metal clanging violently, vibrations humming through my bones like a struck gong.

"You walked away from me!" he growled, face inches from mine, eyes red-rimmed and wild, tears mixing with sweat on his cheeks.

"You walked first," I spat back, blood bubbling on my lips.

Our eyes locked then, and time fractured. The wind died. My heartbeat thundered in my ears. The world narrowed to just us, and in his gaze I saw the boy again, the scared kid on the riverbank, feet dangling in cool water, dreaming of escape from the nothing that defined us. The pain there was ancient, a wound never healed, festering into the monster before me.

He went for my throat, fingers like vise grips, squeezing air from my lungs. Black spots danced in my vision, the night sky tilting. I shoved him back with everything left in me, twisting his arm until tendons screamed, forcing him to his knees with a pained cry. He fought like a caged beast, snarling, teeth bared, fists swinging wildly, one catching my kidney in a kidney punch that doubled me over, nausea surging hot in my throat.

But I refused to fall. Not here. Not to him.

I drove my shoulder into his chest, lifting him off the gravel and slamming him down with a bone-jarring thud that echoed across the roof. He rolled, coughing wetly, blood streaking his mouth and chin, gravel embedded in his cheek like shrapnel.

I staggered toward my pistol near the edge, fingers numb and shaking as I scooped it up, the cold metal heavy in my palm. I turned back, leveling the barrel at him.

He tried to stand, but his legs buckled, causing him to drop to one knee. He looked up, no fire left in his eyes, just a hollow, shattered emptiness that mirrored the void in my own chest.

"So, this is it," he whispered, voice barely carrying over the wind, tears carving clean tracks through the grime on his face. "Do it. End me."

My finger curled around the trigger, trembling. The weight of it all crashed down, years of brotherhood, betrayal, blood, tearing me apart from the inside, chest heaving with sobs I could not hold back.

"You're my brother, Jesse," I said, voice breaking into pieces. "I can't kill you."

His breath hitched, a sob escaping him as something deep inside him finally shattered. His shoulders shook; his head bowed in defeat.

"Why couldn't I have been more like you?" he murmured, voice raw and small, like the boy he once was. "Why couldn't I have been better?"

I took a step closer, the pistol lowering slightly. He flinched but did not pull away, eyes meeting mine one last time, filled with regret that cut deeper than any wound.

Before either of us could speak again, engines roared from below, two trucks screeching into the alley, doors flying open, armed Klansmen spilling out like shadows came alive, rifles glinting under streetlights.

Jesse glanced over the edge, his face draining of what little color remained.

"They're here for us," he said quietly, voice hollow with resignation. "And they won't stop until both of us are in the ground."

I tightened my grip on the pistol, the cold wind slicing across my sweat-drenched skin, raising gooseflesh. For the first time in years, Jesse looked truly terrified, eyes wide, breath shallow, and in that moment, staring down at the men who had twisted us both, I had no idea how to save either of us.

CHAPTER THIRTY

The trucks skidded to a halt in the alley below, tires screeching against the wet pavement. Doors slammed like gunshots, one after another. Heavy boots pounded the ground, echoing up the brick walls. I crouched at the rooftop edge, heart hammering, and watched them pour out, white-robed figures spilling from the shadows like ghosts in the streetlight, rifles and shotguns already raised. Their voices cut through the night, sharp and hateful: "Spread out! Check every exit!"

Their long shadows stretched and twisted across the alley walls as they fanned around the building, blocking every door, every corner.

Jesse stood beside me, gripping the ledge so hard his knuckles went white. His jaw trembled, but he clenched it tight. No tears, just a raw, burning shame in his eyes, like he was swallowing poison he had brewed himself.

He whispered, voice low and cracked. "They're here to clean house."

I could not answer. Blood roared in my ears. My fingers tightened around the grip of my pistol until the metal bit into my skin. On any other night, under different stars, Jesse might have been down there with them, hood up, rifle ready. But tonight, he stood with me. Tonight, he was mine to protect, no matter what we would both become.

The rooftop door below rattled hard, metal screeching against the frame.

"They're coming up," I said.

Jesse's head snapped toward the stairwell. His hand shook as he snatched the shotgun from beside the vent, the cold steel clinking against his wristwatch.

"You still with me?" I asked.

He swallowed hard. "Just this once."

The door exploded inward with a deafening bang. Muzzle flashes lit the stairwell like lightning. Bullets whined past us, sparking off the gravel and pinging against the metal vents. Jesse and I dove behind the rusted water tank as rounds tore the air, kicking up sharp bits of stone that stung our faces.

"I counted six in the trucks," Jesse panted, breath fogging in the cold. "They will not all come up at once. They will choke the exits first."

I risked a glance around the tank. A man in a dark windbreaker kicked the door wide and stepped out, rifle sweeping the roof. I squeezed the trigger once.

The shot cracked like thunder; blood sprayed hot and bright across the wall as he clutched his throat and collapsed, legs kicking.

Two more rushed out behind him. Jesse pulled both triggers. BOOM-BOOM. The shotgun roared, smoke pouring from the barrels. The men screamed as buckshot ripped into them, sending them tumbling backward down the stairs in a tangle of limbs and blood.

A third appeared in the doorway, yelling into a handheld radio: "Code Black! Both targets alive—repeat, both—"

My second bullet took him in the face. He dropped without another sound.

Jesse stared at me, chest heaving, the smell of gunpowder thick between us. "We gotta move while they're regrouping."

We sprinted across the gravel, boots crunching, the acrid smoke trailing from Jesse's shotgun. We reached the stairwell. The bodies lay sprawled across the landing, blood already pooling dark and sticky, dripping down the steps in slow rivulets. The air reeked of hot iron and fear.

Jesse swept the corners with the empty shotgun. "More on the second floor."

"We push together," I said.

He nodded, no hesitation, no complaint. He moved like a man who had already accepted he might die tonight, as long as he did not die alone.

We stepped into the stairwell. The fluorescent bulb overhead flickered, bathing everything in a sickly yellow pulse. I kept my pistol up; Jesse followed with the shotgun reversed like a club. Halfway down, a door burst open. A Klansman lunged out, swinging a baseball bat wrapped in barbed wire. The spikes whistled past my ear and tore into the wall, shredding plaster.

I ducked. Jesse swung the shotgun stock like a hammer, crunching into the man's ribs. The bat clattered to the floor. I drove my fists into the man's face twice, feeling bone give under my knuckles, then swept his legs and kicked him hard. He tumbled headfirst down the stairs; his neck snapped with a wet crack when he hit the landing.

Jesse scooped up the barbed bat. "I'll take this."

The second-floor hallway stretched ahead, long and dim, lit by a single flickering bulb. Office doors lined both sides like silent witnesses. At the far end, an overturned table formed a makeshift barricade.

Whispers drifted from behind it: "They're coming... both of them... spread out."

I motioned low. Jesse crouched beside me, sweat dripping from his chin, eyes broad and shining. "You ready?" I whispered.

"No," he breathed. "But I ain't got a choice."

We crept forward. Halfway down, gunfire erupted, sharp cracks and the splintering of wood. Bullets sparked off the walls, filling the air with plaster dust that tasted like chalk. We dove behind a doorframe as rounds chewed the hallway apart.

More shouting, boots scraping. I leaned out and fired three quick shots. Someone screamed and fell. Jesse charged across the hall, swinging the bat. It smashed into a rifle barrel, sparks flew, then caught the man square in the jaw with a sickening crunch of bone and teeth.

Two more burst from an office. I tackled one; we crashed through a table, glass, and wood, exploding around us. He grabbed a jagged shard and tried to stab me. I caught his wrist, twisted until the joint popped. He howled. I slammed his head into the floor until the howling stopped.

The other went for Jesse. Jesse grabbed him by the shirt, slammed him against the wall, and pounded the bat into his skull again and again until blood streaked the plaster like red paint.

Jesse leaned on the bat, breathing hard, chest heaving. "They're driving us toward the lobby."

"Then we go through the lobby," I said.

"That's suicide."

"They expect us to run scared. We hit them head-on."

He stared at me, hands trembling around the bat. "You know we can't both make it out."

I stepped past him, sliding fresh rounds into the pistol. "Then we make damn sure at least one of us does."

He swallowed and followed.

We hit the bottom stairs hard; my knees nearly buckled from the impact. My lungs burned; every breath scraped like sandpaper. Jesse landed beside me, bleeding from a gash on his forehead, eyes wild, clutching the revolver he had pulled from his coat. We were both shaking, bruised and cut, shirts torn and soaked with sweat and blood.

The lobby opened up ahead like a trap: an expansive room the size of a small bar. A long wooden counter ran along the left wall, bottles glinting behind it. Round tables and chairs lay scattered and overturned. A pool table sat dead center, green felt already torn. Framed photos of hooded men grinning proudly lined the walls. A jukebox in the corner blinked weakly through cracked glass. The air tasted stale, with notes of old beer, cigar ash, and now the fresh scent of gunpowder.

Then they came.

White robes, some still fastening their hoods, others bare-faced but wearing the same pale hatred in their eyes. Shotguns, rifles, and pistols were shoved into belts. Too many. Far too many.

Jesse swallowed hard. "We ain't making it unless we move now."

I stepped out and fired three shots, crack-crack-crack. One dropped instantly. Another stumbled behind a table, clutching his leg. The rest roared and opened fire. Bullets tore into the staircase pillars, showering us with wood splinters that stung like hornets.

I ducked as the world exploded, bottles behind the bar shattering, glass raining down in glittering shards. Jesse fired over my shoulder and yelled, "Left—they're flanking!"

I slid down the last steps and rolled behind an overturned chair. A rifle barrel poked around the bar corner. I shot it point-blank; the man toppled over the counter with a crash, blood pooling among the broken glass.

They spread out in pairs, using the same tactics I had once been taught. Quick sweep, box the target, force the crossfire. Of course they did.

Jesse met my eyes across the chaos. He was bleeding through his shirt, but still here, still fighting.

"Follow my lead," I whispered.

He nodded once.

I bolted for the pool table. Bullets chased my heels. One grazed my thigh, hot and searing. Jesse dove behind a nearby table. The Klansmen formed a half-circle, closing in.

One climbed onto the bar for a better angle. I put a bullet in his chest before he could aim at Jesse. He fell backward into the liquor shelves, bottles burst like fireworks, whiskey and glass pouring down.

Another rushed Jesse's table, firing wildly. Wood exploded around him. Jesse rolled clear, snatched a pool ball, and hurled it. It struck the man's jaw with a wet crack. Two teeth skittered across the floor as he dropped, screaming.

A pump shotgun boomed; the pool table above me shredded. I crawled underneath, grabbed a broken cue, and waited. Boots thudded closer. I burst out and drove the jagged end into a man's throat. He gagged, clutched the wood, and collapsed, choking.

Another swung a bat at my head. I ducked, caught his arm, and twisted until the bone snapped. He screamed; I kicked his knee sideways, and he crumpled.

Behind me, Jesse fired again and again. The room filled with smoke, shouts, and the coppery reek of blood.

Two more charged from behind the bar with knives flashing. I grabbed him by the coat and slammed his head into a pillar. He went limp. The second slashed my shoulder, fire racing across my skin. I swung a heavy brass spittoon into his face; he dropped soundlessly.

But more kept coming, pouring in from the front doors.

Jesse and I locked eyes. We both knew we had to break out now or die here.

I crawled to a cluster of overturned chairs and crates. Jesse slid behind the bar. Our breath came in ragged gasps; sweat and blood stung our eyes.

Three men lined up in the center, rifles steady.

Jesse shouted, "Caleb—down!"

I flattened as they opened fire. The pool table legs shattered; dust choked the air. I rolled and fired blindly. One dropped. Jesse vaulted the bar and shot another twice in the chest.

I sprinted low through the wreckage to the wall by the front door. It was chained shut. No give.

Jesse yelled my name. A huge Klansman had him from behind, club raised. The blow caught Jesse in the rib. He wheezed and dropped to one knee.

I shot the attacker in the leg, then the chest. He fell. I grabbed Jesse's collar and dragged him behind a tipped table as bullets chewed the wall above us.

"You good?" I gasped.

He nodded, pain twisting his face. "Just keep me alive long enough to kill Ezekiel myself."

I gave a grim smile. "Then we do it together."

For a second, he just stared, something soft breaking through the fear. Then he nodded.

I spotted a narrow hallway behind the bar. "That way."

I hauled him up. We moved, half-dragging, half-running, bullets kicking up splinters around our boots. I fired right, dropping two men closing in. Jesse fired left-handed, teeth bared, picking off shadows.

Two more blocked the hallway door. I charged the first, slamming him into the wall; his wild shot blasted the ceiling. I elbowed his jawbone, which shifted sickeningly. Jesse headbutted the second and emptied his revolver into the man's gut. The body slid down the wall.

More shouts behind us, reinforcements flooding the lobby.

Jesse grabbed my shirt. "Go—now!"

We shoved through the door into a dim storage room stacked with old chairs and yellowed pamphlets. We slammed it shut. I threw my shoulder against the handle while Jesse reloaded with shaking fingers. The door shuddered as bodies rammed its wood, splintering, hinges screaming.

Jesse limped to the far window overlooking the back alley and smashed the glass with his revolver butt. Cold night air rushed in.

"Caleb—this way!"

The door cracked wide; a hand forced through. I fired point-blank. The hand vanished in a spray of red.

Jesse climbed out first, boots scraping the sill. I followed, dropping into the alley as the door behind us exploded open.

We ran.

Blood pounding in our ears, lungs burning, legs screaming, but alive. Side by side through the darkness. Like brothers. For the first time in days, like real brothers.

CHAPTER THIRTY-ONE

The lobby reeked of gunpowder and fresh blood, thick and metallic, clinging to the back of my throat. The constant ringing in my ears muffled everything, making the world feel distant and dreamlike. As we burst outside, the cold night air slapped my face like an icy hand, sharp and stinging. I gulped it down, desperate for oxygen that did not taste like smoke. The street stretched out dimly under a few buzzing streetlamps, their weak yellow glow casting long shadows. But it was enough to spot the dark shapes gathering more Klansmen, dozens of them, more. They swarmed from the backs of trucks, emerged from narrow alleys, and stepped out from behind parked cars like ghosts rising from the fog. For a split second, the whole scene froze, the night air thick with tension, as if everyone were holding their breath, waiting for the first move.

Jesse wiped a smear of blood from his split lip and spat it onto the cracked sidewalk. His breaths came in ragged gasps, matching my own. Every muscle in my body ached, bruised, and stiff. If I stopped now, I would collapse in a heap. He glanced at me, his eyes meeting mine, and in that look, all our shared history-the good, the bad, the broken-pulsed between us like a single heartbeat. I gave a slight nod back. Then the gunfire shattered the silence.

I dove behind a rusty old sedan parked at the curb, the metal cold and gritty under my hands. Bullets cracked against the pavement, sending sparks flying and shards of asphalt stinging my skin. Glass from the car's windows exploded in a shower of fragments. Jesse slid in next to me, shattering the remaining window with his elbow and firing back through the frame. The heat from passing rounds brushed my cheek like a hot wind, too close for comfort. Someone barked orders in the distance. Another voice screamed in pain. I popped up just high enough to squeeze off two shots, then ducked as a shotgun blast ripped a jagged hole through the trunk, the boom vibrating through my chest.

We could not stay pinned down. The cars were flimsy covers, and they would surround us in seconds. Jesse tapped my arm, his fingers sticky with blood, and pointed across the street to a narrow alley. It looked dark and tight, but it could funnel them into a choke point. I waited for a lull in the firing, then bolted, my legs wobbling under me as adrenaline surged. Jesse followed right behind, and we slipped into the alley just as bullets slammed into the brick wall where we had been, chunks of mortar crumbling like dry earth.

The alley stank of rotting garbage and stagnant puddles, the sour rot making my stomach churn. Toppled trash cans blocked parts of the path, and rats skittered over splintered wooden crates, their tiny claws scratching against the concrete. The faint glow of the streetlights faded quickly, leaving us in near darkness. Our boots echoed loudly off the walls. Behind us, heavy footsteps pounded; they were already chasing. The first pursuer rounded the corner, and I spun, slamming him hard into the rough brick. His rifle clattered to the wet ground with a metallic ring. Jesse snatched it up while I wrestled the man down, pinning him with my knee and cracking the butt of my pistol against his temple until he went limp.

We pushed deeper, the alley curving sharply. At the far end, another group blocked our way, their silhouettes backlit by distant lights. Jesse fired first, the rifle's crack echoing like thunder in the confined space. They scattered, diving for cover, and returned fire. Bullets chipped bricks inches from my cheek, sending sharp fragments into my skin. I flanked left and slid behind an overflowing dumpster, its rusted sides cold and slimy. Jesse crouched beside a stack of rotting crates and laid down bursts of suppressing fire. Muzzle flashes lit the alley in strobing bursts, casting wild, flickering shadows on the walls.

One of them charged unthinkingly toward Jesse, boots splashing through puddles. I stepped out from cover and met him head-on. We collided with a bone-jarring thud, my shoulder screaming in protest. I used his momentum to flip him onto the ground, the impact knocking the wind out of him. Jesse shot the man creeping up behind him, the blast close enough that I felt the heat. The alley thundered with gunfire until it fell silent again, save for the endless ringing in my head.

We had to keep moving. We were still trapped like rats. Jesse pointed to the far wall, where a fire escape ladder hung just out of reach, its rusted rungs glistening with dew. I cupped my hands into a step, and he planted his boot in them. Grunting with effort, I boosted him up until he grabbed the bottom rung. He climbed fast, metal creaking under his weight, then reached down to haul me up, his grip strong despite the blood on his palms. We were halfway when more Klansmen flooded into the alley below. Shots ricocheted off the fire escape's frame with sharp pings. One grazed my arm, fire slicing my skin, followed by warm blood trickling down.

We scrambled faster. Jesse reached the platform first and yanked me onto it, the grated metal biting into my knees. We sprinted across the walkway, the whole structure shaking, and jumped down into the next alley. This one opened onto the back street, but engines roared nearby, trucks circling, headlights sweeping like searchlights. They were trying to trap us from both sides.

Jesse cursed under his breath, bending over a nearby dumpster and ripping open its lid with a screech of metal. Inside, amid the trash, were old cleaning supplies: bottles of bleach and glass jars filled with a volatile substance. He grabbed two jars and stuffed them into his jacket pockets. When he looked at me, his eyes held that wild, reckless half-smile I had seen only a handful of times, like the old Jesse, the one who had always pushed the edge. I knew trouble was coming, but it was the kind that might save our skin.

We crept toward the alley's mouth. The trucks swung into view, their headlights blinding, beams cutting through the smoke. Men leaped from the beds, rifles at the ready, boots thudding on pavement. Jesse pulled out the jars, yanked a lighter from his pocket, and flicked it once, twice, until a small flame danced. He touched it to a rag stuffed in one jar, and it ignited with a whoosh, flames licking the glass.

They spotted him a second too late.

Jesse lobbed the first jar underhand. It arced through the air and shattered under the lead truck with a crash. The explosion was sharp and contained, but it ignited leaking fuel from the engine. Flames erupted under the chassis, rolling out in a wave, and seconds later, the whole truck burst into a violent fireball. The heat blasted us like an oven door opening, and men screamed as flames swallowed those too close. Jesse hurled the second jar at the rear truck. It exploded similarly; the shockwave shoved us back a step, singeing my eyebrows.

Chaos erupted. Men yelled and scattered, some firing blindly through the thickening smoke. I picked off targets in the confusion, the pistol bucking in my hand. Jesse did the same. The street turned into a nightmare of roaring fire, shadows dancing, and echoing gunfire.

Then it quieted, the only sounds the crackle of flames and distant shouts. Smoke drifted like fog, ash falling softly like black snow. My chest heaved with every painful breath. Jesse leaned against a lamppost, gripping his shotgun like a crutch, his body swaying.

I walked over and clapped a hand on his shoulder. He looked up, exhausted, worn to the bone, but alive. We didn't need words; we just shared a long, silent glance.

We stepped out into the open street together. The burning trucks lit the block in flickering orange, flames crackling hungrily. In my mind, I braced for more men, more guns, more death. But the night stayed still, except for the fire's glow. We were alive. Somehow. And the fight was not done.

The flames from the wrecked trucks bathed the street in harsh orange light, thick smoke rolling across the pavement like low storm clouds. It twisted around fallen bodies and glinted off shattered glass scattered like diamonds. My ears rang from the blasts, but I caught snippets: distant shouts, boots slapping asphalt, the clatter of metal weapons. They were regrouping and coming back for more.

I wiped soot from my stinging eyes and raised my rifle again, arms trembling so hard I braced them against a cold streetlamp pole. Jesse pushed himself upright beside me, hacking up smoke, his face a mask of blood and grime. The firelight carved deep shadows across him, making him look like a ghost risen from hell. But he stood tall, and that was enough.

He pointed down the street, voice rough. "They ain't done, Caleb."

"I know," I said. "Neither are we."

Dark figures emerged through the haze, rifles up, charging with furious shouts. The first one fired wildly, the bullet whining past my ear. I squeezed the trigger and dropped him mid-stride. Jesse pumped his shotgun and blasted another who got too close, the buckshot's roar echoing off buildings. More poured from the alleys. It felt endless, like an army from the shadows.

We backed up slowly, fighting every step of the way. Time blurred into a haze of noise, pain, and fire. I lost count of the kills. A Klansman lunged from my left; I swung my rifle like a bat, cracking it across his jaw with a wet crunch. He crumpled, blood spraying the pavement. Another grabbed me from behind, arms like vices. I slammed my elbow into his ribs repeatedly until he gasped and loosened. Spinning, I shot him point-blank, the heat of the muzzle flash warming my face.

Jesse handled two at once: he smashed one's face into a car hood with a denting thud, then stabbed the other in the thigh with a jagged piece of metal from the debris. They kept swarming, but he fought like a cornered animal, ferocious, with nothing left to lose and everything to protect.

Gunfire cracked from the block's far end. "There they are!" someone yelled, and bullets ripped toward us again.

I grabbed Jesse's jacket. "Move!"

We dove behind a stone planter box, bullets chipping the brick overhead, dust raining down like gritty snow. My cheek slammed the pavement, stars exploding in my vision. Jesse fired blindly over the top and cursed as his gun clicked empty.

"Reload," I said.

"My hands ain't working right," he muttered, fingers fumbling.

"I got it." I tossed him fresh shells and leaned out, dropping two more with quick shots. But four replaced them. The street felt like it was closing in, walls tightening. We were exhausted; they were not. Another group flanked from the side. I ducked behind a bullet-riddled mailbox as rounds punched through the thin metal.

Jesse stumbled next to me, dropping to one knee, blood trickling down his arm in a dark stream. I yanked him behind a parked truck. "Stay with me," I growled.

He laughed weakly, breathless. "Ain't going anywhere."

A metallic clink hit the pavement nearby. "Grenade," I whispered.

I hauled Jesse and threw us both behind the truck's thick engine block. The explosion rocked the world, dust billowing from the roofs, and windows rattling. The shockwave punched my ribs like a hammer, and for a moment, my hearing vanished in a high-pitched whine.

We could not hide forever. We had to turn the tide. "We rush them," I said.

Jesse stared like I had lost my mind. "You sure?"

"Dead sure."

He grinned through bloodied teeth. "Alright then."

We exploded from cover together, smoke cloaking our charge. I fired until my rifle emptied, then switched to my pistol, the recoil jarring my wrists. Jesse scooped a fallen gun and sprayed the line of retreating men. Bodies hit the ground hard. The survivors turned to flee, which proved to be their fatal error.

We pursued adrenaline, fueling my screaming muscles, as my lungs burned like fire. I crashed into the nearest one, tackling him down and punching until he went still. Jesse slammed another into a lamppost with a resounding crack. More shouts echoed. Footsteps pounded.

One final wave surged from an alley, six or seven, hard to count in the haze. I raised my pistol. Jesse lifted his rifle. We charged once more.

Gunfire erupted in a final frenzy. A round grazed my cheek, hot and stinging. Jesse took one in the shoulder but kept shooting, gritting through the pain. Two fell. Then another. One got close with a crowbar swinging. I dodged, elbowed his throat until he gagged, and Jesse finished him off.

The last two leveled their rifles. I dropped one. Jesse got the other. Then... nothing. No more shouts. No running. No shots. Just the hungry crackle of flames eating the trucks and the whisper of ash settling on the street.

I staggered back to the hood of a charred car and slid down against it, legs giving out. Jesse limped over and collapsed beside me. We sat in the fire's warm glow, chests heaving, barely alive.

He looked at me. "We did it," he said softly.

"Yeah," I whispered. "We did."

We sat for a long moment, the heat from the flames soothing our faces while the cold night nipped at our backs. Blood crusted on our clothes. My hands shook uncontrollably; I pressed them against my knees to hide it.

Jesse stood first, wincing with every movement. He offered a hand, and I took it, letting him pull me up. We gripped each other's shoulders.

"Guess this is where we part," he said.

"Guess so."

He paused. "Caleb... thank you."

I shook my head. "Thank you."

We pulled into a rough hug, two battered men, reeking of blood and smoke, holding onto the last shreds of our bond. When we stepped back, words failed us.

Jesse turned toward the dark end of the street and limped away, fading into the shadows. I headed the opposite way, into the night. The flames behind us burned bright, then dimmed to an orange flicker in the distance.

CHAPTER THIRTY- TWO

Jesse Boone limped along the deserted city street, his palm clamped tight over the warm, sticky wound in his side. Blood seeped between his fingers, slow and relentless. The distant crackle and heat of the earlier fires had faded, giving way to the harsh, yellowish glow of streetlamps that hummed with a low, incessant buzz overhead. His heavy boots scuffed roughly against the cracked pavement, grinding bits of grit and glass underfoot. Each labored step sent a sharp jolt of pain through his body, a constant echo that he should have died hours earlier, or perhaps days, or even years. Exhaustion blurred the timelines in his mind. He had no strength left to sort them out. His thoughts drifted aimlessly, seeking refuge in memories.

Mary Beth. The gentle curve of her smile. The light, musical ring of her laugh. The soft warmth of her trust in him. The bitter sting of how he had let her down. Isaiah, gasping on that dusty farmhouse floor, blood pooling dark and thick around him. A young boy, he never intended to harm. A boy whose wide, terrified eyes still burned into his soul.

Caleb. His brother. His enemy. His brother once more. The contradiction twisted inside him, impossible to unravel. Lily. Pure and kind, far too gentle for the violence of this life. Far too good for the ruined world that men like him had helped create.

And Ezekiel. The mentor who molded him with iron hands. The manipulator who exploited him without remorse. The one who discarded him the instant everything unraveled.

Jesse drew in a ragged breath that rasped wetly in his throat, tasting copper on his tongue. What remained of him now? He searched for a name to fit the hollow shell he had become. Something shattered beyond repair. Something adrift and forsaken. Something caught in the gray space between sinner and sufferer. Something utterly unworthy of redemption.

He paused at the entrance to a narrow alley and slumped against the rough brick wall, its cold, gritty surface biting into his back as he fought for air. The night air hung still and heavy, carrying faint scents of rain-soaked asphalt and distant smoke. The battle had ended. Relief should have washed over him.

Instead, a vast emptiness filled his chest. Then, soft footsteps echoed from the street behind him, steady and deliberate.

Jesse raised his head, peering through the hazy dimness. A tall figure emerged at the end of the block, cloaked entirely in black fabric that absorbed the light. A deep hood concealed his face in shadow. He advanced with unwavering intent, his movements silent and fluid, betraying no trace of doubt or hesitation.

Jesse's pulse slowed to a heavy thud in his ears. His breath snagged in his throat. That familiar outline sent ice through his veins. He pushed himself upright, a fiery stab ripping through his cracked ribs. "You," he breathed, the word barely audible. The figure continued forward without pause.

Jesse's trembling hand fumbled for the pistol wedged against the small of his back. Weariness slowed his fingers, turning simple motion into agony. He had scarcely wrapped them around the grip when the figure blurred closer with unnatural swiftness.

A glint of steel caught the lamplight. Two sharp, suppressed cracks split the quiet night. Jesse reeled back, shock widening his eyes. Fresh heat bloomed across his chest, soaking rapidly through his shirt. He pressed a hand there, feeling the slick warmth spread beneath his palm. His lips parted, but only a faint gasp escaped. His legs gave way, and he crumpled to the sidewalk as the ground seemed to lurch beneath him.

A final, shuddering exhale escaped him, soft and fractured, as he slumped against the unforgiving chill of the concrete.

The hooded figure loomed above the fallen body for a long moment, still as stone, gaze fixed downward as if committing every detail to memory. Then he pivoted silently and approached the old pay phone bolted to the corner wall.

He lifted the receiver, its plastic cool against his gloved hand. A coin clinked into the slot. He dialed a memorized sequence. The line connected with a faint click. A voice answered on the other end. The hooded figure spoke in a low, even tone. "It's done."

EZEIKEL POV

The chandelier above the Whitlock dining room cast a golden haze over the long mahogany table, its crystals tinkling softly whenever the ceiling fan stirred the air. Candle flames danced in silver holders, throwing flickering shadows across the starched white linen. The scent of roasted lamb and rosemary lingered, mingling with the faint sweetness of blackberry pie cooling on the sideboard. Fine china gleamed, forks and knives aligned with military precision. The Boone family sat opposite their hosts, faces flushed from wine and laughter, plates pushed aside after second helpings.

Ezekiel leaned back in his chair at the head of the table, his voice still warm from the tall tale he had spun about outrunning federal agents in a moonlit cornfield years ago. Mrs. Boone pressed a lace handkerchief to her damp eyes, shoulders shaking with residual chuckles. Mr. Boone lifted his crystal glass in a lazy toast, the ruby port catching the light. For one fragile moment, the room felt like any respectable Southern home on a quiet evening, as if the blood and burning crosses outside these walls belonged to another world entirely.

Ezekiel's smile was wide and effortless, the kind he could hold for hours without a single muscle twitching out of place. At the opposite end, Annabelle sat perfectly composed, her gloved hands folded in her lap, spine straight against the high-backed chair. Her lips curved upward in the polite half-smile expected of a gracious hostess. Nothing in her pale blue eyes betrayed the chill that had settled in her chest the moment the Boones arrived.

Then the telephone rang.

The shrill bell sliced through the room like a straight razor. Laughter died instantly. Glasses paused halfway to lips. Even the candles seemed to flicker in alarm. Ezekiel's smile locked in place for the briefest heartbeat before he rose with fluid calm.

"If you'll excuse me," he said, voice smooth as polished marble. He stepped into the shadowed hallway, footsteps muffled by the thick Persian runner.

He lifted the heavy Bakelite receiver. Silence stretched for a second on the line. Then the voice, low and familiar, delivered the words he had paid for in blood and favors.

"It's done."

Ezekiel's eyelids drifted shut. A slow breath filled his lungs, steadying the sudden thunder in his veins. "Understood," he answered, barely above a whisper. He set the receiver back in its cradle with deliberate care, as though the click might echo back into the dining room and betray him.

He paused in the dim hallway, facing the gilded mirror above the console table. In its reflection, he adjusted his expression the way a tailor pins a suit: brows drawn together in sorrow, mouth softened, eyes glistening with unshed tears. Shoulders rounded just enough to suggest unbearable weight. When he turned back toward the light, the mask was flawless.

He reentered the dining room, gripping the doorframe as if his legs might give way. The Boones looked up, concern already etching their faces.

Ezekiel's voice cracked like thin ice. "I am so sorry." The words trembled in the sudden hush. "So terribly sorry."

Mrs. Boone's handkerchief lowered. "Ezekiel? What's happened?"

He pressed one hand to the back of a chair for support, knuckles whitening. Tears welled and spilled in perfect, glistening tracks down his weathered cheeks. "It's Jesse," he said, the name breaking in his throat. "Your boy... he's gone. Murdered. By my own son. By Caleb."

The sound Mrs. Boone made was not quite human: a sharp, keen animal muffled against her palm. Her body folded forward as though an invisible fist had struck her stomach. Mr. Boone surged to his feet, chair scraping harshly against the hardwood. His glass tipped, port bleeding across the white cloth like a fresh wound. He gripped the table edge, veins standing out on his forearms, staring at Ezekiel as if the words refused to settle in his mind.

The room filled with their grief: raw, choking sobs from Mrs. Boone, the ragged breathing of a father trying not to shatter. Ezekiel moved forward and gathered the weeping woman into his arms, one hand cradling the back of her head with practiced tenderness.

"I swear on everything holy," he said, voice thick with manufactured rage, "the Klan will not rest until Caleb pays. We will hunt him to the ends of the earth. Your boy will be avenged."

Mrs. Boone clung to him, tears soaking into his crisp white shirt. Mr. Boone sank slowly back into his chair, eyes fixed on nothing, face drained of color.

Annabelle remained motionless at her end of the table. Her fork lay untouched beside congealing slices of lamb. The candlelight caught the faint tremor in her lower lip, the only outward sign of the revulsion churning inside her. She had watched him rehearse this exact performance in their bedroom mirror a dozen times. She had seen him wield grief like a blade in dimly lit rooms where men confessed secrets they later regretted. But never so brazenly. Never over dinner with grieving parents who still believed him a friend.

She knew every tear was calculated. She knew Jesse's blood stained her husband's hands far more than Caleb's. Yet she sat in silence, gaze dropping to the crimson stain spreading across the tablecloth. Her gloved fingers tightened imperceptibly in her lap.

Tonight was not the night to speak the truth. Not without proof. Not when Ezekiel's web was still perfectly spun.

So, she lowered her eyes and said nothing, while the man she had once loved held two broken parents and wept tears that belonged to no one but himself.

CHAPTER THIRTY THREE

A few weeks slipped by like gentle tides, each day weaving a fragile thread of normalcy into the fabric of survival.

The California sun dipped low over the Pacific coastline, painting the sky in molten gold and blushing oranges that reflected off the endless blue. Waves rolled in with a rhythmic hush, their foam whispering secrets to the golden sand as seabirds wheeled overhead, crying out in lazy arcs. The air carried the briny tang of salt, mingled with the faint, earthy scent of kelp drying on the shore and the distant aroma of grilled fish from nearby bonfires. It was a world alive with quiet renewal, far removed from the shadows that had once chased them.

Lily Jefferson pushed through the creaky screen door at the back of the weathered beachfront restaurant, her fingers deftly tying the strings of her faded apron around her waist. The lunch rush had ebbed an hour earlier, leaving the dining room empty save for the soft patter of her sneakers on the worn wooden floor. Sunlight slanted through the salt-crusted windows, casting warm pools across the mismatched tables. Isaiah was safe at school; his backpack stuffed with seashells he had collected on the beach that morning. For the first time all day, the world breathed easy around him, hurried orders, no clatter of plates, just the distant crash of surf and the occasional squawk of a gull scavenging for scraps.

She dipped her rag into a bucket of soapy water, the lemon-fresh scent cutting through the lingering grease of fried calamari. Wiping down a sticky tabletop, she hummed a half-remembered lullaby under her breath, the soft and tentative melody. This was her new life: a borrowed name, a rented room above the restaurant, air that tasted like freedom instead of fear. Some mornings still jolted her awake, heart pounding with phantom echoes of gunfire or heavy boots on gravel or Caleb's urgent whispers in the dead of night. But those ghosts were fading now, dissolving like mist in the morning sun. Slowly. Painfully. With a stubborn hope that rooted deeper each day.

She turned to snag a fresh rag from the counter and froze, her breath catching in her throat.

He stood framed in the open doorway, silhouetted against the blazing afternoon light. Caleb.

His dark hair had grown out a touch, tousled by wind and neglect, curling slightly at the nape of his neck. His clothes, faded jeans and a threadbare flannel shirt, hung loose on his frame, worn thin from endless roads and hidden skirmishes she could only imagine. Stubble shadowed his jaw, etched with lines of exhaustion and unspoken burdens. But those eyes... those warm, hazel eyes that had anchored her through the darkest storms, they had not changed. They shone with a quiet vulnerability, locking onto hers like a lighthouse beacon.

Lily's heart slammed against her ribs, a wild drumbeat that drowned out the waves. Emotions crashed over her in a dizzying torrent: the fierce ache of love she had buried deep, the sharp sting of fury at his absence, the sweet rush of relief, the heavy sorrow of lost time, the bubbling joy of reunion, the tender heartache of what they had endured. It all collided in her chest, stealing her words and threatening to buckle her knees.

Caleb lifted a hand in a hesitant wave, his callused palm catching the light. A shy grin tugged at the corner of his mouth, boyish and familiar despite everything. "Excuse me, ma'am," he drawled, his voice light but laced with that Southern warmth she craved, "I was wondering if this place serves up any food... or if y'all specialize in emotional devastation these days?"

Lily blinked, her lips parting in stunned silence. She tried to speak to yell, to whisper, to anything, but her throat tightened around a knot of unshed tears.

Caleb tilted his head, nodding solemnly as if pondering her mute expression. "Is that the scientific term for the face you're making right now? Cause if so, I reckon I qualify as exhibit A."

A laugh burst from her then, raw and unbidden, half giggle, half sob that tore straight from her soul. It echoed off the empty walls, mingled with the distant roar of the sea. Tears spilled hot down her cheeks as she pressed a hand to her mouth, but nothing could hold her back. She ran to him, bare feet slapping the floor, apron strings fluttering behind like wings.

Caleb caught her mid-stride, his strong arms encircling her waist with effortless strength. She buried her face in his chest, inhaling the familiar scent of him, road dust, faint soap, and that indefinable something that was purely Caleb. Sobs wracked her body as she clutched his shirt, fingers twisting in the fabric like she feared he would dissolve into the ether.

"Please," she whispered against him, her voice muffled and trembling, "please don't ever leave me again. Don't leave us."

Caleb's hold tightened, his own breath hitching as he pressed his cheek to her hair. The faint tremor in his arms betrayed the storm raging inside him: guilt, longing, and the fierce protectiveness he had carried like armor. "I won't," he murmured, voice rough with emotion, his lips brushing her temple. "I swear it, Lily. I promise on everything we hold dear. I will never leave you or Isaiah again. We are done running. This is home now, you, me, him. Together."

She pulled back just enough to search his face, her hands cupping his stubbled cheeks. His eyes were rimmed red, glistening with unshed tears that mirrored her own. Raw honesty shone there, stripped of pretense. No more shadows. No more goodbyes.

Lily smiled through the blur of her tears, a radiant, bone-deep smile that lit her from within. "Welcome home, then," she said softly, her thumb tracing the line of his jaw.

They stood like that for long moments, wrapped in each other's arms as the sun dipped lower, bathing the room in an amber glow. Outside, the waves continued their eternal rhythm, salt-kissed wind drifting through the doorway carrying the promise of fresh starts. Isaiah would be home soon, bursting through the door with stories and sandy shoes, his laughter filling the spaces between them. They would build something real here, on the porch watching the sunset, lazy weekends chasing crabs along the tide line, quiet nights where love healed what violence had broken.

For the first time in what felt like forever, amid the golden haze of a California evening, the world did not just feel gentle. It felt whole. Redeemed. Full of the simple, heartwarming miracle of second chances.

The end.

CALEB WHITLOCK WILL RETURN.

ABOUT THE AUTHOR

Toby Lamar Yawn is an author from Mobile, Alabama. Toby yawn was born on July 21, 1991. Toby Yawn was adopted at one year old and moved to the

Austell, GA, in Cobb County. Toby attended school at Austell Elementary, where he studied under his favorite Elementary teacher, Ms. Erin Paul. Toby would move to Hiram, Ga. He attended Hiram High School. In the 11th grade, he discovered his love of writing while in Mr. Bob Banks' English class. In the 12th grade, he found his passion for storytelling in Mrs. Troy's English class.

Mr. Yawn has always been passionate about movies and books. Especially the works of Ian Fleming and JK Rollings. Toby yawn is a big fan of Tim Pool, Ben Shapiro, Michael Knowles, Matt Walsh, and Andrew Klavan. He is also a big fan of Star Wars.

Mr. Yawn is currently working for Walmart while attending Bellevue University online.

www.ingramcontent.com/pod-product-compliance
Lightning Source LLC
LaVergne TN
LVHW020718110826
845149LV00012B/2317

* 9 7 9 8 9 9 4 4 1 8 8 1 9 *